She was dressed ~~like~~ one of Santa's helpers.

Amanda stood just inside the doorway of Josh Larkland's messy, high-tech office. He examined her as if he'd never seen a woman before.

Since he was being so rude about it, Amanda didn't feel guilty scrutinizing him. Josh Larkland was one of the most gorgeous men she'd ever seen.

His gaze met hers. "I'm staring, aren't I? It's a natural reaction, you know. After all, I've never seen an elf before." He looked a little puzzled by that, as if he couldn't understand why dozens of Santa's helpers weren't lurking about.

"I'm not really an elf, you know. I—"

"Oh, I know. They don't exist." His eyes gleamed with admiration. "But if they did, they would look exactly like you."

Amanda's stomach fluttered. *Don't get involved with the clients.* "Look, Mr. Larkland…"

"No one around here calls me Mr. Larkland, not even my secretary. It's probably a sign of disrespect." He smiled that charming smile.

Don't get involved, she reminded herself.

Josh took a step toward her. "Shall we begin with who's been *naughty* or *nice*…?" His smile was both naughty and nice.

Don't get involved, she recited.

Too late!

Dear Reader,

Ho, ho, ho! 'Tis the season for jolly St. Nick, chestnuts roasting over an open fire and mistletoe carefully hung in *strategic* doorways (kissing, after all, is a very serious matter). It's also a great season for LOVE & LAUGHTER. We're celebrating with two wonderfully funny, always entertaining and very romantic holiday books.

Temptation favorite Alyssa Dean spins a tale of mischief, family and the true meaning of Christmas in *Mistletoe Mischief*. As Josh professes frequently, he doesn't mind the yuletide season, he just doesn't have time for it! I think you'll be just as delighted with Josh Larkland's Christmas turnaround as he is!

Debbi Rawlins writes about a different type of Santa, a Santa undercover. Santa is really Jill Tanner, a woman on the run for her life who ends up hiding out in the last place she would expect—a suburban home that's missing a very crucial element, a mother. Try getting out of that conundrum and baking Christmas cookies at the same time! Debbi continues to delight her fans with stories for Harlequin American Romance.

Wishing you all the joys of the holiday season (and lots of good presents!),

Malle Vallik

Malle Vallik
Associate Senior Editor

MISTLETOE MISCHIEF
Alyssa Dean

Harlequin Books

TORONTO • NEW YORK • LONDON
AMSTERDAM • PARIS • SYDNEY • HAMBURG
STOCKHOLM • ATHENS • TOKYO • MILAN
MADRID • WARSAW • BUDAPEST • AUCKLAND

ISBN 0-373-44033-2

MISTLETOE MISCHIEF

A funny thing happened...

A lot of unexpected and funny things have happened to me while celebrating Christmas, but I fondly recall the year my boss went away for the holidays. (This was before my full-time writing career began.) While he was gone, we walled up the door to his office with nice wooden paneling. When we were finished, you couldn't tell there had ever been an office there. (I've got great pictures of this.) He was so surprised when he came back to work and discovered that his office was missing. I don't think it was the Christmas present he'd been expecting.

But it is just the sort of present my hero, Josh Larkland, would be receiving from his employees if he hadn't found his very own Christmas elf. I hope you enjoy *Mistletoe Mischief* and the holiday season!

—Alyssa Dean

Books by Alyssa Dean

HARLEQUIN TEMPTATION
524—MAD ABOUT YOU
551—THE LAST HERO
636—RESCUING CHRISTINE

Don't miss any of our special offers. Write to us at the following address for information on our newest releases.

Harlequin Reader Service
U.S.: 3010 Walden Ave., P.O. Box 1325, Buffalo, NY 14269
Canadian: P.O. Box 609, Fort Erie, Ont. L2A 5X3

For
my mother, Phyllis
and my Grandma King.
Two people who taught me
the real meaning of Christmas.

1

"CHRISTMAS ELVES!" Brandy snorted.

She indignantly marched into the vestibule of Amanda's apartment and stomped the snow off her boots onto the welcome mat. "Whose brilliant idea was it to advertise ourselves as Christmas elves?"

Amanda took a sip of coffee while considering the question. "Mine, I suppose. I thought it might attract attention." She picked up one of their flyers from the coffee table and read it out loud. "'Problems coping with Christmas? Call the Christmas Elves at A&B Executive Services. We provide everything the busy executive needs to have a Merry Christmas.'"

"I think it needs a disclaimer!" Brandy kicked off her boots, stormed into the living room, and flopped down onto the couch beside Amanda.

"What's wrong with it? It's lively and different, and...and we both do sort of look like elves." At least they were both on the short side, although Amanda thought Brandy's curly brown hair, green eyes and cuddly-looking figure was more elf-like than her own shoulder-length blond hair and slender build. She studied Brandy's face. "Although right now you look more like a wee cranky leprechaun. What's wrong?"

"Mr. Denton is what's wrong."

"Mr. Denton?" Amanda watched Brandy tug off

her jacket and toss it over a chair. "From Denton Accounting?"

"That's him." Brandy curled her legs under her. "You would not believe what that busy executive thought he needed to have a Merry Christmas!"

"Oh, no," said Amanda. "He didn't…"

"He did." Brandy shuddered. "Right there in his office. I asked him what I could do to make his Christmas merrier and he…lunged at me."

"Lunged at you?" Amanda looked over at her friend with concern. "Are you okay?"

"Yes. No." Brandy rubbed a hand across her forehead. "I don't know. Is there any more coffee?"

"Sure." Amanda stood and went into the kitchen to pour Brandy a mug and carried it into the living room. "Now tell me everything that happened."

"There's not much to tell." Brandy took a couple of sips and settled back into the cushiony back of the floral couch. "I arrived, Mr. Denton ushered me into his office, poured me a cup of coffee, and the next thing I knew, he had his hands all over me."

"That's…dreadful!"

"That's what I thought!" Brandy made a face. "I mean, at nine o'clock in the morning! If it had been an afternoon appointment I might have been expecting it, but in the morning? Most men are hardly awake, and this chunky little bald guy is all ready to rock and roll?"

Amanda almost giggled at Brandy's outraged expression. "That's peculiar, all right," she agreed. "Go on. What did you do?"

Brandy's lips twitched into a smile. "Well, actually it was kind of funny, Amanda. Mr. Denton is as short and chubby as I am. He touched, I shoved…it was sort of like being a participant in a midget sumo wrestling contest.''

Amanda smiled at the image, then almost immediately sobered. ''Who won?''

''I did, of course. I have three older brothers who are a lot tougher than Mr. Denton.'' Brandy raised one perfectly groomed eyebrow. ''Besides, as soon as I smacked him, he got the message and backed off.'' She sighed. ''I don't want to be pessimistic here, but I'd say we aren't going to get a whole lot of business from Denton Accounting—especially after Mr. Denton explains his bruise to Mrs. Denton...and all the little Dentonites.''

Amanda had almost forgotten what this meant to their business in her concern for Brandy. ''That's fine with me,'' she said firmly. ''We don't need *that* kind of business.''

''I suppose not,'' said Brandy. ''Although *some* business would be nice.'' She took another sip of coffee. ''You know the real scary thing, Amanda? For a moment I was actually tempted to go along with Mr. Denton.''

Amanda's jaw dropped. ''What?''

''I was.'' Brandy actually blushed. ''He lunged and this thought flashed through my mind that if that was what it was going to take to get our business off the ground, maybe I should do it.''

Amanda was horrified. ''Brandy!''

''Then I realized that if Mr. Denton touched me I'd throw up, and that wouldn't do one thing for our business, either. So I just smacked him and left.''

''Good,'' said Amanda. ''We aren't that desperate.''

Brandy raised an eyebrow. ''We're pretty close.

We've been in the executive services business for three months, and you can count our clients on my ring finger.''

Amanda squirmed. That was pretty close to true. Business hadn't been anywhere near what they'd projected. ''We've had more than that,'' she reminded them both. ''We did that thing for the Claire Foundation.''

''You didn't charge them anything more than cost!''

Amanda winced. ''They're a charitable organization. It didn't seem right…''

''We're *not* a charitable organization.'' Brandy took another gulp of coffee. ''And then there was that Bernard Trucking thing. You raced all over town lining up corporate gifts for him to hand out—and we ended up paying for them.''

Amanda winced again. ''He was such a nice man. And he really couldn't afford…''

''We couldn't afford it! And Mr. Bernard might have been a nice man but his son sure wasn't. You ended up dating Eddy Bernard! He borrowed a couple of hundred dollars from you and hasn't called you since.''

Amanda squirmed and bent her head. She didn't like thinking about Eddy. ''I'm sure he'll pay me back when he gets his feet on the ground,'' she murmured, although she'd be surprised if that happened.

''And what about that Higgins Stainless Steel thing?'' Brandy continued. ''They almost begged us to take their business and you refused.''

''I don't feel one bit guilty about that,'' Amanda announced, narrowing her eyes. ''Lenny Higgins was pond scum. Besides arranging the Higgins's Christmas party, he wanted me to buy his mistress a Christmas present so his wife wouldn't find out. That isn't right, Brandy. For one thing, he shouldn't have had a mistress. And for another, if he wanted to buy her a present he should have picked it out himself.''

''I suppose you've got a point,'' Brandy admitted. ''But you can't keep getting personally involved with the clients, or we'll never make any money.'' She sank even deeper into the cushions, then sighed. ''Maybe we aren't cut out for this business. You're too soft-hearted and I just seem to attract weirdos.''

''You don't…''

''Yes, I do. Look at the business I've brought in. First there was that fellow who wanted us to arrange the 'Welcome Winter' frolic in the park.'' She snorted. ''Remember how his little group wanted to welcome winter? If we hadn't caught on in time, we'd have ended up in jail!''

''True, but…''

''Then there was that group of insurance adjusters whose idea of a Christmas party was having me pop out of a Christmas cake. Me, for heaven's sake! Do you know how much icing it would take just to cover me up?''

Amanda pictured her partner covered in white gooey icing and giggled.

''Now I get Mr. Denton,'' Brandy continued. ''What is it about me, anyway? Aren't men supposed to prefer tall, leggy blondes, not short, dumpy brunettes?''

Amanda shook her head at that. Brandy might not be classically beautiful but there was a come-hither sparkle in her green eyes and her ample-bosomed figure had always attracted male attention. ''You might

be short, but you aren't dumpy,'' Amanda decided.
''There's something kind of…earthy about you, I
think. Men just look at you and think naughty
thoughts.''

''That's for sure,'' Brandy groaned. ''Every man I
meet wants to drag me into a bedroom.''

''And every man I meet thinks I'm a sucker,''
Amanda complained. That did seem to be the way
her relationships went. She lent men money, did their
laundry, got all involved in their problems…and then
they'd decide they didn't need her.

Brandy was instantly sympathetic. ''You're not a
sucker, Amanda. You just…pick the wrong men and
get too involved with people. And it's a good thing
for me you're like that. I don't know what I would
have done without you after Charlie and I split up.
Starting this business gave me something else to think
about,'' she said, sighing sadly. ''I just wish it was
going to work.''

''Of course it's going to work,'' Amanda insisted
with a lot more confidence than she felt. ''It has to,
Brandy. I don't have many other alternatives.''

''We could always go back to the temp agency.''

Amanda shuddered at the thought. ''No thanks.
I've had enough of spending days at copy machines
or filing papers—and so have you. We were both full-
time secretaries before the world got into this down-
sizing kick. We're great at arranging things.''

''We could try to get permanent jobs.''

''I don't want to do that, either,'' Amanda objected.
''Even if we could find jobs, which is pretty doubtful
these days, we'd just get terminated in the next down-
sizing. We're always the first to go.''

''It's because we're short,'' Brandy complained.

"When someone says down, people think of us. It always makes me feel like one of those ducks in the shooting gallery."

"I don't want to do it again! I don't want to work for anyone else. I want to work for myself."

"So do I, but I'd like an income while I do it." Brandy pushed aside a few strands of hair that were tickling her face. "I never thought we'd have this problem. After all, there aren't that many executive services companies in Calgary."

"It's probably because we aren't known," Amanda suggested. "When people want someone to handle office parties, and seminars, or to arrange a tasteful little business luncheon, they don't think of A&B Executive Services. If we could just get our foot in the door…"

"We'll find some weirdo or moocher on the other side?" Brandy guessed.

Amanda frowned at her. "No, we won't. There has to be some nice, normal, busy executive who is awful at dealing with Christmas. All we have to do is find him."

JOSH LARKLAND was dealing with Christmas in his own way—he was trying to ignore it.

Unfortunately, it wasn't ignoring him.

"Christmas!" he grunted.

He dropped the phone receiver into the cradle and gave it the scowl it deserved. That did it. If one more person said the C-word to him any time within the next ten years, he was going to scream.

He massaged his temples and looked longingly at his computer. That's what he should be doing today—working on the design for his voice response unit.

That's what his computer hardware company—Lark-land Technology Development—did, and that's what Josh wanted to be doing. Instead, he'd spent a good portion of the morning talking to people about un-important things that all had something to do with Christmas!

It had started with a phone call from his aunt Mimi at nine o'clock this morning. "It's not a Christmas party, Josh. We're just having a few people over to-night, under the umbrella of a Christmas theme. You will come, won't you? The whole family will be here, along with some of your uncle Reg's business friends and a few neighbors. Oh, and Marple Stevens is com-ing. She's got such a lovely daughter. You really should meet her."

That had been followed by a call from his stepsis-ter, Charmaine. "It's my annual Universal Christmas Grandiola. You should come. My friend Stacey is go-ing to be in from Detroit. You really should meet her."

Then there had been his aunt Louise. "We haven't seen you for such a long time. Do come. Frank's part-ner's friend's husband's cousin is going to be here. You really should meet her."

If it wasn't relatives calling, it was business ac-quaintances—potential investors who wanted him to make an appearance at their Christmas party, or to ensure that they were invited to his. Current investors who wanted much the same thing.

And to top it all off, his mother!

Now he really wanted to scream.

Josh thought for a second, then decided to do it. "Ma-aa-bb-bl-ee!" he bellowed.

He waited for a moment, and when no one showed up he did it again. "Mable!"

There was silence, followed by a huge, dramatic sigh and the squeak of a chair. Finally Mable appeared in his doorway, her large, square figure blocking most of the light from the reception area. "Do you want something or are you just trying to annoy me?"

"Yes, I want something. I want a one-way ticket to January."

"Of course," said Mable. She took a few steps into the room. "Would that be economy or first-class?"

"I'll go baggage if you can do it. And make sure no one else is on the plane. The rest of the world can stay in December, since they all seem to like it so much."

"My, my!" said Mable. She strolled closer and plunked her ample figure into the one visitor's chair Josh allowed in his office. "We're really getting into the Christmas spirit this year, aren't we?"

"No, we aren't." Josh lowered his eyebrows. "And it's not because there's something wrong with me. I like Christmas well enough. I just don't like it right now!"

Mable smiled. "I'm afraid you're simply going to have to cope. Christmas isn't something I can reschedule."

"Why not?" Josh picked up a pencil and twirled it around his fingers. "This happens every year. Christmas comes along and it's never convenient. If they have to have these sorts of holidays, why don't they do it some other time?"

"I don't know. I guess they just don't consider your schedule when they plan these things."

"They certainly don't." Josh caught the twitch of her lips and his irritation increased. "Did you find that place yet, like I asked you to?"

"It was more like a royal command, and no, I didn't. It's almost impossible to find a place to have a Christmas party now! It's the first of December. Everything has been booked for months."

"That's just great." Josh tossed the pencil onto his desk. "According to Hank Turnbull, I have to host one of these Christmas things. He said it would be the perfect opportunity to show my hardware to potential investors. How can I do that if you won't find a place to have it?"

Mable stared right back at him. "Don't you blame this on me, Josh Larkland. I wouldn't have had any problem finding a place if *you* had thought about doing this a couple of months ago."

"I was busy a couple of months ago." Josh gestured at the papers littering his desk. "And I'm busy now, too. I've got networks to design, schematics to check…equipment to test. I don't have time for this Christmas stuff."

"It's not that bad. It just…"

"It's worse than that bad! It's a pain in the neck." Josh stretched back a hand to massage that part of his anatomy. "People have been phoning all day, suggesting we 'get together before Christmas.' A stack of invitations for me to go places came in the mail. Just thinking up reasons not to go is a full-time job!"

Mable's smile widened. "Why don't you just go to some of them? Most people enjoy…"

Josh shuddered at the thought. "Well, I don't. I hate those things. No one ever talks about interesting stuff like network throughput and voice response learning curves. They just sit around, laughing... talking...drinking. Sometimes they even...sing!''

Mable clamped her lips together, and her shoulders shook. "How...uh...bizarre."

"It sure is." Josh folded his arms and glowered at the world. "Besides, most of these Christmas things are put on by *my* relatives."

Mable rolled her eyes. "There's nothing wrong with your relatives, Josh. Apart from the fact that you have an awful lot of them, they all seem like nice people."

"They probably are." Josh got out of his chair and wandered over to look out the floor-to-ceiling windows behind his desk. There really wasn't anything wrong with his family, and it wasn't that Josh didn't like them. He was actually very fond of them, when he remembered they existed. However, none of them knew anything about electronics, telecommunications, robotics or remote voice activation, which was all Josh was interested in talking about. So he couldn't think of a single reason why he should leave his office early to drive across town just to spend an evening pretending to listen to them while he thought about something else.

Besides, they all had a bad habit of delivering little lectures to him about issues he didn't consider important. "They just...don't approve of my life-style or something."

Mable snorted. "Of course they don't approve of your life-style! *I* don't approve of your life-style." She paused. "Not that I consider the way you live much of a style."

"Jeez!" Josh turned to give her a warning glare,

and wondered how much trouble it would be to get a new secretary. "Not you, too!"

"Yes, me, too." Mable held up a palm. "Don't get me wrong. When you try, you can be a remarkably decent person. You just don't...pay much attention to your life."

Josh furrowed his brow. "What is that supposed to mean?"

"Well...you spend most of your waking hours either in the lab or this office."

Josh took a quick look around. The room was exactly as he liked it—a sofa in a corner so he could catch a few hours' sleep when he worked all night, a computer on his desk, and another unit on the big table beside it. "What's wrong with my office?" he asked. "It's just the way I like it. We're a high-tech—"

"I know, I know. And there's no question you're a supreme techo. But you really don't have much of a personal life." Mable sighed and shifted in the chair. "For example, I've never known you to date the same woman any longer than a week—and that only happens if she keeps phoning you!"

"Yeah, well..." Josh rubbed an eye. That seemed to be everyone's big complaint. If they weren't urging him to bring some woman home to meet them, they were dredging up women for him to meet. Sometimes they even hinted that he should be doing this himself.

Josh didn't grasp the logic of that. There were plenty of women in his family already. They didn't need any more. He certainly didn't need one. Oh, he liked women well enough, and when he was with one, he enjoyed himself. But they weren't as interesting or as important as the high-tech industry he was trying to develop.

"And then there's your family," Mable went on. "You don't spend much time with them, either."

"I spend lots of time with them," Josh insisted, although he had a funny feeling that wasn't really the case. "Besides, when I do see them, they take turns dragging me into a corner and telling me what's wrong with me. It's almost a tradition. If we could just eat turkey like everyone else, it might not be so bad." He returned to his chair and settled into it. "Now they've come up with this...this present thing!"

Mable looked bewildered. "What present thing?"

"You know. Christmas presents."

"Oh, that." Mable shrugged a shoulder. "You don't spend a lot of time on that, Josh. Every year you do the same thing. You buy a case of perfume and a case of brandy. Men get brandy. Women get perfume." She put her head to one side. "Which reminds me. Can I get on the brandy list this year? I've still got three bottles of perfume."

Josh rolled his eyes. "I'm not giving you perfume this year. Or brandy, either."

"Why not?"

"I don't know," Josh said irritably. "My mother just said that she didn't think it was appropriate."

"Your mother?" Mable glanced at the phone, then back at him. "That's right. She just called, didn't she?"

"Uh-huh."

Mable blinked twice. "She phoned to tell you that she doesn't think it's appropriate to give me perfume?"

"It's not just you. It's everyone. She suggested I do something a little more personal."

Actually, it had been more than a suggestion. "I want to talk to you about Christmas," she'd started. Then she'd gone into one of her unfathomable mother-type lectures about thoughtfulness and the real meaning of Christmas that had contained a whole bunch of "not appropriates" and "It doesn't have to be expensive, dear. But something a little more personal would be better." And when he'd said he wasn't sure he could "do" personal, she'd said in that case it might be better if he didn't give them anything at all!

It had almost sounded good—except something in his mother's voice told Josh that if he said, "Okay, fine, I won't," his mother would be really upset. And although she, along with the rest of his relatives, drove him crazy at times, he didn't like it when she was upset.

"She doesn't think giving everyone the same thing is very thoughtful."

"Ah," said Mable. "Well, she does have a point."

"She does?" Josh peered at her. "What is it?"

"Well, it isn't very thoughtful. It's sort of like…Christmas shopping in bulk."

Josh didn't see the problem. "What's wrong with that?"

"It's just not done. If you're going to give someone a present, it should mean something. You don't just do it to get it over with."

"Oh," said Josh. He studied her face for a moment. Mable was probably good at this sort of thing—certainly a lot better than he was. "Well, since you understand it, how about if you…"

Mable shook her head. "There's no way I'm doing your Christmas shopping for you. For one thing, I don't have time, and for another, I don't do things like that."

"Jeez, Mabe!" Josh shoved an exasperated hand through his hair. "It's not as if I'm asking you to have my children. I just want you to pick up a few things."

"You want me to do more than pick up a few things. You want me to think up presents for—how many is it?—a couple of dozen of your relatives. I wouldn't have a clue how to do that."

"Neither do I," Josh muttered. That was the problem. He had no idea what his relatives would consider appropriately personal, and he didn't know how to find out, either. "Couldn't you just…"

"No, I couldn't."

Josh gave her his best I'm-totally-helpless-without-you look, accompanied by a smile. "Please? I really need some help and…"

"No." Mable pushed herself out of the chair. "There's no point in wasting all that charm on me, either. I'm not going to do it, and that's final. I'm your administrative assistant, not Santa Claus."

"Right about now I'd settle for one of his elves," Josh mumbled. He eyed Mable hopefully. "How about getting me one of them?"

"Sure, why not?" Mable turned to leave. "Right after I find a place for your Christmas party and arrange for a ticket to January." She chuckled. "Actually, getting you an elf might be a whole lot easier."

IF MABLE WAS GOING TO find that elf, she'd better do it soon, Josh decided a few hours later.

He sat at his desk and stared blindly at his computer screen. At least the afternoon had gone a little better than the morning. He'd given Mable firm instructions that he wasn't to be disturbed, and, for once, she'd actually carried them out. He'd had a good four hours without any interruptions.

But he hadn't accomplished anything. This whole present thing bothered him a lot more than he liked to admit. He had the distinct impression from his mother that it was important to her as well as to everyone else. It was one of those things the rest of the world seemed to understand, while he fumbled around, trying to figure out what was going on.

And, if he was going to be honest with himself, he'd have to admit that he didn't try very hard. He did care about his relatives, and he didn't like being the focus of their disapproval. But he had a business to run, inventions to invent, investors to line up. He didn't have time to worry about this sort of thing. What he needed was someone to handle all this Christmas stuff—the parties, the invitations, as well as producing a nice batch of personal Christmas presents, all gift-wrapped and labeled, without him having to do anything about it.

He'd just thought that when his office door opened and Mable stepped in. "I think I've found a solution to one of your problems," she said.

Josh eyed her warily. Her lips were stretched into a wide smile, and there was a definite twinkle in her eye. "Oh?" he said.

"Yes." Mable's smile grew. "I talked to a friend of mine who suggested I call an executive services agency. So I did."

"And?"

"And they sent someone right over." She turned toward the door. "Come on in, dear. And don't let Mr. Larkland's manner put you off. He's horrible, but he's harmless."

Josh opened his mouth to object, then closed it again and blinked with startled surprise at the woman entering his office. She stood about five-five, with shoulder-length, white-blond hair that curled around her face. She was wearing a dark green skirt, a long red jacket and high-laced black boots. "This is Amanda Kringleton," Mable announced. She strode across the room and handed Josh a piece of red paper. "Your Christmas elf."

2

TERRIFIC, thought Amanda. *This time I got the weirdo.*

She stood just inside the doorway of Josh Larkland's messy, high-tech office and wished Brandy was with her. However, Brandy had been out when Larkland Technical Development called. The woman on the other end of the phone had sounded perfectly normal. Amanda had been positive she could handle it by herself.

Now she wasn't so sure. It wasn't that the president of Larkland Technology Development had done anything to make her think he wasn't a nice, normal person. He hadn't said anything, either. All he had done was stare at her.

He wasn't even subtle about it. He leaned back against his desk, absently stroking his chin with one hand while he examined her from head to toe and back up again as if he'd never seen a woman before.

Since he was being so rude about it, Amanda didn't feel guilty scrutinizing him. She probably would have done it anyway, because Josh Larkland was one of the most attractive men she'd ever seen. He was just under six feet tall, with mussy curly brown hair, deliciously deep brown eyes framed with thick, dark lashes, and a high-cheekboned, square-jawed face that was almost classically handsome. The sleeves of his pink-and-gray-striped white shirt were rolled up to his elbows, his tie was bundled up in a corner of his desk instead of tied neatly around his neck, and the blue suit jacket that matched his pants was thrown over the back of his chair in a manner that invited wrinkles.

Okay. He was a good-looking, well-dressed weirdo who didn't take care of his clothes, wasn't hung up on neatness and had never seen a woman before.

Amanda took a deep breath. She could handle this. All she had to do was act cool and professional and...

His gaze met hers. He blinked several times, then moved his lips into a slow smile that was so charming Amanda forgot all about acting cool and professional. "I'm staring, aren't I?" he asked.

"Well...uh...yes, I guess you are," said Amanda.

"I thought so." He shrugged. "It's a natural reaction, you know. After all, I've never seen an elf before." He looked a little puzzled by that, as if he couldn't understand why dozens of Santa's helpers weren't lurking about. Amanda glowered at the flyer in his hand. Darn those things. As soon as she left this office she was going to find them all and burn them. "I'm not really an elf, you know. I..."

"Oh, I know. They don't exist, right?" His eyes gleamed with admiration. "But if they did, they would look exactly like you."

Amanda's stomach fluttered. *Don't get involved with the clients,* she reminded herself. *Stick to a professional approach.* This guy was charming, but he could still be a creep on the make. She cleared her throat. "Look, Mr. Larkland..."

He waved that aside. "Josh. No one around here calls me Mr. Larkland, not even Mable. It's probably a sign of disrespect." He frowned. "So is her telling you I'm horrible. I'm not *that* horrible. Today was an exception. And now that you're here, I'm positive I'll be in a much better mood.''

Amanda almost lost herself in his eyes and his smile. He might be on the make but he wasn't a creep. As a matter of fact...

''I guess we should get down to business, hmm?'' Josh motioned her toward the single black leather visitor's chair in front of his desk and strolled around to the chair behind it. ''What do you need to get started?''

Amanda struggled to remember what business she was in. ''I, um...''

''I guess you'll require a list.'' He stretched back in his chair, blinked up at the ceiling, and started reciting names. ''Let's see. There's my mother, of course. Edwina Davidson. She married Harold after my father died, which is why our last names aren't the same. Then there's my sisters, Shelby, Marilla, and Charmaine. They're actually my stepsisters, I suppose, since they're Harold's children. Oh, and my aunts—Judith, Francine, Sofia, Louise, and Mimi. Francine is my mother's sister. Sofia is my father's sister, and Louise and Mimi are Harold's sisters. Judith is their aunt. That makes her a stepsomething, but I can never remember...'' He looked over at Amanda and stopped. ''Shouldn't you be writing this down?''

Amanda had been listening in bewildered silence as he listed off his relatives. Now she snapped to attention. ''I could but...'' Was she missing something or was he simply not making any sense? ''I was, um, under the impression that we were talking about a business function.''

Josh looked puzzled. ''A business function?''

"Yes. Your secretary said that you wanted to host a Christmas party...a *business* Christmas party."

"Oh, that." His eyes widened. "You can do that, *too?*"

"Of course." Amanda was starting to feel a little dizzy. "That's what A&B Executive Services does. We arrange office parties, organize business seminars..."

"And handle this Christmas present thing, too? That's...amazing."

"Christmas presents?" Amanda rubbed her forehead with a finger in a vain attempt to understand. "Well, um, we do handle a small line of corporate gifts. Coffee-table books. Business-card holders..."

"Don't you buy those in bulk?" asked Josh.

"Sometimes. But..."

"Then I don't think they'll work for my family."

"Your family?" Amanda stared at him in astonishment. Surely he wasn't suggesting... "You want me to get Christmas presents for your *family?*"

"Of course I do. Isn't that why you're here?"

Amanda was immensely disappointed in him. He was just like other executive types she'd run into—so absorbed in their work that they didn't have time to spend on the important things in life. "No, it isn't. I'm here to discuss your office Christmas party."

"But what about these Christmas presents? You can do that, too, can't you?"

There was a hint of desperation in his eyes. Amanda hesitated. He did look as if he needed help... She needed the business and it wouldn't hurt to...

It certainly would hurt. Brandy would be horrified. "No," said Amanda. "That's not really something A&B Executive Services does."

"It isn't?"

"No, it isn't," Amanda said firmly. "Besides, Christmas presents are something people should really handle themselves."

"Yeah?" He blinked a couple of times as if unclear on the concept. "What if they don't have time? Couldn't you just—" he made a vague, sweeping motion with one hand "—do it?"

Amanda hesitated. He looked so helpless... They desperately needed the business and...

And buying other people's Christmas presents had to be on Brandy's list of "getting too involved." Amanda gave him a small, cool smile. "I don't think so. Now, if we could get back to discussing your Christmas function...."

"My Christmas function." Josh stretched back in his chair and studied her. "Okay. Let's talk about that."

Amanda suddenly felt uneasy. There was something about the glint in his brown eyes that made her nervous. "Well, um, your secretary told me that you were having difficulty finding a place to host a Christmas party. She's right. I couldn't find a place, either, so I suggested you do it here. With a little work we could make the place look festive. Serve drinks...hors d'oeuvres. We could have a different theme for each floor...get in a string quartet..."

"That sounds interesting." Josh tapped his fingers together. "Tell me, Amanda... I can call you Amanda, can't I? Or do I have call you Ms. Kringleton?"

"Amanda is fine."

"Okay, Amanda. Exactly how many of these sorts of functions have you organized?"

"Me, personally? Quite a few actually. I..."

"I meant A&B Executive Services."

"Not a great deal," Amanda admitted after a pause. "We've only been in the business a few months, and…"

"Ah," said Josh. "I see."

Amanda looked into his face and got the distinct impression that he did see. He might not bear a strong resemblance to an efficient corporate executive, but she began to feel that he was not a man who should be underestimated.

Josh picked up a pencil and stroked it across his bottom lip. "It's a difficult business to break into, isn't it?"

Amanda watched the eraser end of the pencil move across his mouth and sucked in her own bottom lip. "It, uh, can be."

"Uh-huh. What you really need to get business is a track record, and to get a track record, you need business. Right?"

Amanda considered lying, caught the sparkle in his eye, and didn't. "Yes," she said.

"Arranging the Larkland Christmas party might be just the sort of thing you need, hmm?"

"It would certainly help."

"I would think so," said Josh. He was silent as he studied her. Then he spoke again in a silky smooth voice. "How about if we make a deal, Amanda?"

Amanda eyed him suspiciously. She was pretty sure she knew what was coming. "A deal?"

"Yeah." He dropped the pencil and leaned forward, forearms resting against the end of the desk. "You handle this Christmas present thing for me, and you can have the Larkland Christmas party business."

Amanda swallowed. "That sounds a little like blackmail, Mr. Larkland."

"Josh." He grinned. "And it isn't blackmail at all. I believe it falls more under the heading of extortion. However, I'm desperate, I have a feeling you are, too, and this way we could help each other." He blinked in his deceptively innocent fashion. "And I'm not suggesting you do it for free. I'll pay for your time."

"Are you sure you can afford it?" Amanda retorted. "Considering how many relatives you have..."

"Oh, good," said Josh. "You do have a sense of humor. I was starting to wonder."

Amanda watched his lips move into that slow, sexy smile and felt herself melt. It was a bad sign. Josh Larkland was the epitome of the work-absorbed executive. He was twisting her arm to get her to do something she didn't want to do, and she still liked him.

"Don't worry about the money," Josh added. "I can afford it. And this is an opportunity you can't afford to pass up. There'll be a lot of people at the Larkland Christmas thing—important people who I'm sure spend enormous sums on arranging... arrangements." He grinned. "If you do a good job, you could end up with enough business to keep you going for a while."

He was right about that. And maybe it wasn't such a big deal. All she had to do was handle his Christmas shopping. How hard could that be? Brandy might not like it, but she would be pleased that Amanda had landed a job that they'd get paid for—and that it didn't involve icing. "All right," she said. "I suppose I could pick up a few things."

"And gift wrap them?"

"And gift wrap them."

"How about Christmas cards? Can you send those?"

Amanda felt as if she were sinking into quicksand. "I suppose I could…"

Josh gestured at a stack of envelopes on the corner of his desk. "And you'd have to go through all these invitations and send some sort of response. Something that says no without sounding as if it means 'There's no way in hell.'"

"Oh," said Amanda. She eyed the mound. "Well, um, okay, I guess I…"

"Good." Josh settled back into his chair with a satisfied smile. "You're hired."

"YOU CAN'T POSSIBLY be related to all these people," Amanda argued.

She stared at the list of sisters, aunts, uncles and cousins in stunned disbelief. "There are over twenty people on this list. You can't be related to all of them," she said, dropping the list onto her lap. She had been seated in the uncomfortable and only chair in his office for the past hour and would have given anything to get up and stretch her legs.

"Twenty?" Josh thought about it. "Did I mention Mable?"

"No."

"Well, make it twenty-one. And yes, I am related to most of them, except for Mable of course." He frowned. "It's my mother's fault. She married Harold without giving any consideration to the problems that was going to cause me at Christmas."

"I imagine she had other things on her mind at the

time,'' Amanda murmured, trying to surreptitiously stretch one leg, then the other. Ah, that felt better!

"I suppose," Josh agreed, and Amanda found herself wondering if he had the slightest idea what any of those things might have been. After an hour with him, she'd concluded that Josh Larkland was the most clued-out man she'd ever met...and perhaps the most irresistible. His aura of helplessness, along with his physical attractiveness and incredible charm, would stop any woman in her tracks.

So why didn't he have a woman around to handle his shopping for him?

That's none of your business, Amanda scolded herself. She was not getting personally involved with this guy. Still, she couldn't help wondering...

She focused her attention back on his list of relatives. "At least most of these people are women. I can get them gift baskets filled with soap and perfume and..."

"Perfume?" Josh shook his head. "Perfume is out."

"Why?"

He shrugged a shoulder. "It just is, that's all. I want something more...personal."

"Personal?" That was the last thing Amanda had expected to hear. "You want me to get these people something personal?"

"That's right," said Josh. "I think it would be more...thoughtful."

"Thoughtful." Amanda struggled to hold back a giggle. "Thoughtful is not when you coerce someone else to do your shopping for you."

Josh grinned right back at her. "Hey, extortion

takes a lot of thought. Especially when you've never done it before.''

"Right." Darn, he was cute. It was almost a shame that he wasn't a creep on the make. Amanda shoved aside the thought and tried to concentrate on the task at hand. "Personal thoughtful presents, hmm. Okay. Well, suppose you tell me something about these people.''

"Like what?''

"Something that would help," Amanda explained. "What they do. What they like." Josh still looked blank. "Why don't we start with your sisters? How old are they?''

"How old?" Josh's forehead furrowed while he considered it. "I don't know exactly. A lot older than me.''

Amanda wasn't certain if his idea of "a lot" was two or twenty-two. "Would that make them over forty?''

"Not all of them." He stared into the space over her head. "Marilla might be. There was some sort of party in the summer that had to do with forty. I think it was Marilla's birthday…unless it was for her husband. He's really old. Or was it was Frank and Louise's anniversary?''

At this rate she'd be over forty by the time Josh figured it out. Amanda decided to abandon the age angle. "Let's forget that. How about what they do.''

"What they do?" Josh looked as puzzled by that as he had been by their age.

"For a living," Amanda prompted. "What do your sisters do for a living?''

"Well…um…Shelby does something with children.''

"A teacher?" Amanda guessed.

"Either that or a hairdresser," said Josh. "I can never remember. Charmaine works in a bank or a hospital, and Marilla has something to do with animals. She shows them or trains them or..." He shook his head. "I'm not positive. I just know she likes cats."

At last—a decent suggestion. Amanda wrote "cats" beside Marilla's name. It wasn't a bad hint. She could always find some kind of cat ornament. "How about Marilla's husband—" she scanned her list "—Tom?"

"Tom? Oh, he likes cats, too."

Amanda decided she'd heard enough about Marilla and Tom. "What about your other sisters—Shelby and Charmaine? What do they like?"

"I have no idea," said Josh.

No one could know this little about his family. "You must know," Amanda insisted. "Just think. When they get together, what do they talk about?"

Josh shrugged his shoulders. "Nothing in particular. Except for Marilla and Tom. They talk about cats."

Amanda was beginning to form a pretty weird picture of his family, all sitting mutely while this Tom and Marilla lectured on about felines. "Let's try someone else." She scanned her list again. "How about your aunts, Mimi and Louise. Tell me about them."

"There isn't anything to tell! They're my aunts, that's all. And I don't know how old they are!"

Of course he didn't. As a matter of fact, Amanda was starting to wonder if he even knew what his relatives looked like. ''What about your mother? Do you know anything about her?''

Josh's cheekbones reddened. ''Of course I know something about her! She's my mother. Her name is Edwina Davidson. She's been married twice—first to my father. Then to Harold.''

Amanda frowned. ''I need more than that.'' She sat up straighter in the uncomfortable chair.

''I don't know anything more than that!'' Amanda rolled her eyes and Josh scowled. ''Don't look so disapproving. I don't think people should know a whole bunch of personal information about their relatives. It's too…''

''Personal?'' Amanda guessed.

''Exactly!''

Amanda looked down at the list resting on her lap, then back up at him. ''I can't do this.''

''What do you mean, you can't do it? You…''

''No, I can't! I don't think anyone could. It's utterly impossible.''

''It can't be that impossible,'' Josh argued. ''Lots of other people do it. And it's not as if I'm asking you to design a voice-response subrelay. I just want you to get a few presents…''

''Personal presents,'' Amanda corrected. ''For people I haven't met and you don't know anything about.''

They stared at each other. ''Then I guess you'll just have to meet them,'' said Josh.

Amanda couldn't believe her ears. ''Excuse me?''

''You're the one making the big fuss about knowing them,'' Josh observed. ''I'd be perfectly happy if you'd get them something personal without ever meeting them. However, since you're going to be so difficult about it, I guess the only thing to do is to arrange for you to meet them.''

Amanda didn't know what he had in mind, but she was positive she wasn't going to like it. "No," she said. "I am not going to do that. I absolutely refuse to walk up to over twenty strangers and ask them what they want for Christmas. For one thing, I doubt that they would tell me, and for another, they'd probably have me arrested.''

"I wouldn't think so," said Josh. "Elves don't get sent to jail. It would just annoy Santa and no one wants to risk that." She scowled and he held up a hand. "But I'm not suggesting you do that. I don't want my relatives to know about you. I'm supposed to be doing this present thing myself.''

"I guessed that," Amanda muttered under her breath.

Josh ignored her. "What you need to do is meet them…casually. Then you could ask them all kinds of personal questions without them getting suspicious. Sort of like a…a secret-agent elf." He drummed his fingers on his desktop. "Now, how can we arrange that?''

"We can't," said Amanda. "Maybe we should forget this. I—"

Josh interrupted her. "I've got it," he exclaimed. He got up out of his chair and began to pace in front of the windows. "Aunt Mimi.''

"Aunt Mimi?''

"Yes. She's having the whole crowd. Everyone will be there. You can meet them all." He peered at Amanda. "You are free tonight, aren't you?''

Amanda nodded her head, wondering what she was getting herself into. "Great. Then you can go to Aunt Mimi's party."

3

"Aunt Mimi's party?" Brandy repeated incredulously.

She put a hand over her mouth and giggled into it. "This guy actually expected you to go to a family party with him so you could find out personal things about his relatives?"

"That's right." Amanda sat in her kitchen, still a little stunned after her meeting with Josh. "He even hinted that I could go by myself. He said there would be so many people there that no one would notice that they didn't know me and that he wasn't there."

Brandy shook with laughter. "And I thought I'd met them all! What did you say?"

"I talked him out of it!" Amanda felt rather proud of this accomplishment. "After all, they are his relatives. If I have to go, he should have to go, as well."

Brandy's eyes widened. "You're not really going to do this, are you?"

Amanda shrugged. "I have to. If I'm going to get presents for these people, I have to meet them. It's the only way I'm going to find out anything about them." She checked her watch and rose out of her chair. If she hurried, she could have a quick shower. Then there was her hair... "Josh doesn't seem to know much more than their names."

"'Josh,'" Brandy repeated. She followed Amanda

down the hall. "Listen, Amanda, I'm not so sure this is a good idea."

"Why not?" asked Amanda. She went into her bedroom, opened her closet and studied the contents. Josh hadn't been much help in the wardrobe department. "I don't know what anyone wears," he'd said when she'd asked how formal this gathering was. "They just look…clean."

"I just don't," Brandy insisted. She plunked herself on the edge of Amanda's bed. "For one thing, he doesn't sound like the kind of man any woman in her right mind would get near. And for another, he's a client. This morning you were horrified at the idea of me cozying up with a potential client just to improve business. Now you're going to do it."

"I am not cozying up with him!" Amanda objected. Not that she'd mind cozying up with Josh. He was certainly handsome and…

Amanda caught herself. Brandy was right. Josh wasn't the sort of man any woman in her right mind would date. Besides, she wasn't positive Josh would *know* how to cozy up with someone.

She giggled at the thought, then yanked a cherry red knit dress out of the closet. "If anyone is cozying up, it's probably you."

"Me?"

"Yes, you." Amanda turned around. "There are a dozen roses on my kitchen table, along with a card addressed to you."

"Oh, those." Brandy rolled her eyes. "I got those for not cozying up with someone. Mr. Denton sent them."

"Mr. Denton?"

"That character who attacked me this morning,"

Brandy explained. "He sent those along with a card that said 'I'm terribly sorry.'"

"That was nice of him."

"It was, wasn't it?" Brandy considered it for a moment, then shrugged it off. "He's probably just worried I'll call the police...or his wife."

"It was still a nice gesture." Amanda held up the dress. "What do you think of this?"

"It's fine." Brandy's forehead creased in concern. "Are you sure you want to go out with this guy? We don't know much about him. He could be a psychopath or something."

"Josh?" Amanda shook her head. "You don't have to worry about that. And I'm not really going out with him. It's more like I'm...I'm attending a business function."

"Business?" Brandy snorted. "We're in the executive services business, dear, not the executive *dating* services business."

"It's *not* a date!"

"I still don't like it," Brandy said stubbornly. "Maybe I should hang around so I can check him out." She glanced at her watch. "What time is he picking you up?"

"He's not. I'm meeting him there."

"Ah," Brandy drawled wisely. "Yet another gallant gentleman."

"It's not like that!" It wasn't, either. Josh had volunteered to pick her up—after he'd agreed that he should attend, too. Amanda had decided against it. "It's a business function, Brandy. People don't pick up other people to attend a business function. Besides, this made more sense. We both had to change and..."

"What's he changing into?" Brandy interrupted. "A human being?"

"Brandy!"

"We know this type, Amanda. We've both dated men like him. But even they knew something about their mother. This guy sounds like he hardly knows he's *got* a mother."

"He does know he has a mother. He just doesn't know much about her," Brandy said dryly.

Amanda frowned at Brandy. "Don't pick on me. I did what you said to do. I got the business, and I didn't give it away. He's paying full price."

"For what?"

"Well, it's not for me. He's not at all interested in me." She thought about the way he'd looked at her when she'd first walked into this office. He had looked interested. But that was because he wanted her to do all his Christmas shopping for him. "I'm just his...Christmas elf. He sees me as a solution to all his problems."

"And the start of a bunch of yours," Brandy teased. "Listen, Amanda, I do appreciate what you're trying to do, and I want the business as much as you do. But I don't want you to get hurt."

"Don't worry, Brandy. I won't get hurt."

"You will if you get involved with someone like this."

"I'm *not* getting involved with him. I'm going to meet his family tonight, that's all. And we aren't staying long. I'm just supposed to pop in, ask them a whole bunch of personal questions, and pop out. I have to do it fast, because Josh hates those things." She paused. "You know, I feel a little sorry for him.

He's so...clued out. And he sounds completely over-whelmed by his relatives.''

"You feel sorry for him," Brandy repeated. She sighed. "Oh, dear, Amanda. What have you gotten yourself into?''

WHAT HAD HE GOTTEN himself into?

Josh leaned against the archway separating his aunt's living room from the dining room, and took a long swallow of the frothy eggnog punch that Mimi fondly imagined could replace a decent drink. As usual, his aunt had invited three times as many people as she could seat. There were people draped on the sofa, the chairs...even sprawled in front of the fire-place. More than over half were related to him, ninety percent were a good ten years older than he was, and the ones that didn't fall into either of those categories appeared to be women any one of his relatives was trying to set him up with—an intent, narrow-faced woman from Charmaine's cosmic connection class, a perky redhead whom Marilla had introduced as a cat groomer, and a dangerous-looking brunette who was to play the piano later. "So we can sing," Mimi had explained when she'd introduced them.

What in God's name was he doing here?

He took another sip of his drink and analyzed his own question. There were two reasons for his pres-ence—one, so his Christmas elf could find out per-sonal stuff about people, and two, because he was just a little bit uncomfortable with the conversation he'd had with Amanda.

He'd seen the look of disapproval on her face when he'd confessed that he didn't know a whole lot about his relations. He'd been surprised himself at how little he did know. There had been fewer lines of writing on her Christmas gift list than his first plan for his new company. He'd been around these people for most of his life. Granted, he didn't have much in common with them, but shouldn't he know basic details, like how old they were, and what they did for a living?

His musings were interrupted by a middle-aged angular woman wearing a dark blue dress. "Josh?"

"Hi, Mom." Josh bent to kiss her cheek with genuine affection. Come to think of it, he didn't know how old she was, either. He was thirty-two, so she'd have to be somewhere around…

"I'm surprised to see you here," she said. "Especially after our conversation this morning. I thought you might be a little…annoyed."

"Annoyed? Me?" Josh shook his head. "Of course not."

Her gaze searched his face, her blue eyes glimmering with uncertainty. "Then you did understand. About the presents, I mean?"

"Sure," said Josh, although he didn't. He patted her shoulder. "Don't worry. Everything's under control."

"It is?" Edwina looked puzzled, but before she could ask anything, Josh's aunt Mimi bustled up. "Oh, good, Josh, there you are. Marple Stevens has just arrived. She's got her daughter, Freeda, with her." She leaned closer. "Now I want you to be nice to this girl. She owns that little dress shop up on Fifty-ninth. She'd be such a help in your career."

Josh eyed the determined-looking woman entering the living room. "I design voice response systems, Aunt Mimi. It doesn't matter what they wear."

"Ah," said Mimi rather vacantly. "Well, I'm sure she has a nice voice. She sings in the choir, you know."

Before Josh could think of a suitable response, or even decide if there was one, Mimi trotted across the room toward her guests. "Marple, darling, how wonderful to see you. And this must be Freeda. I've got someone here who's anxious to meet you."

Josh groaned and turned, looking for some means of escape, and found himself face-to-face with his uncle Reggie. "Ah, there you are, Josh," Reggie rumbled. "I wanted to have a word with you."

"Did you?" Josh shook Reggie's hand without much enthusiasm. He didn't have anything against his uncle, but he had a strong suspicion that he knew what was coming.

"Yes, I do. Your aunt wanted me to speak to you. She's very concerned about you, you know. So is your mother. And I can understand..."

He went on talking about families and responsibilities and a bunch of other stuff that Josh wasn't interested in hearing. Josh took another sip from his glass. Now he remembered why he didn't spend a lot of time with these people—or know anything personal about them.

He abandoned all attempts to find out anything; his Christmas elf could handle it. She'd better show up soon, too, or he was going to announce that he had developed a sudden case of the plague and get out of here.

AT LEAST ONE of Josh's relatives had the Christmas spirit.

Amanda paid the cabbie, and walked toward the

sprawling bungalow, gaily decorated with an almost obscene number of Christmas lights. There was a large number of cars parked on the street and, as she approached the front door, she could hear music and laughter and the sound of many voices.

She raised a hand to press a finger against the doorbell and hesitated. What on earth had made her agree to do this? It had almost made sense when she was in Josh's office—pop in, ask a whole bunch of personal questions, then pop out. Now it seemed more like an episode of "Mission Impossible."

And, to be perfectly honest, she was a little apprehensive about meeting Josh's relatives. She wasn't sure what to expect—his various descriptions made them sound like either eccentric gargoyles or candidates for sainthood. Besides, in spite of his assurances that no one would notice they had an extra guest, or be upset about it, she felt a little uncomfortable about attending a party to which she hadn't been specifically invited.

She wasn't a party crasher, she reminded herself. She was attending a business function, that's all. Besides, if the noises in there and the number of cars parked on the street out here were any indication of the number of people in that house, there was a good chance no one would notice her. Even if they did, his relatives couldn't possibly be gargoyles, not if they had this many friends.

On the other hand, even gargoyles probably had friends.

Amanda took a deep breath and rang the doorbell. To her immense relief, it wasn't a gargoyle who opened the door. It was a tall, willowy woman with curly salt-and-pepper hair and a friendly smile. "Hello," said Amanda. "I'm Amanda…"

"Amanda! Of course!" The woman opened the door wider. "You must be Hemp's daughter. Do come in." She peered over Amanda's shoulder. "Is your husband not with you, or is he parking the car?"

"No. That is, um, I don't…"

"He couldn't make it? Such a shame. But how nice of you to come on your own. Hemp will be delighted. Come inside, dear. It's getting terribly cold out there, isn't it? Totally unpredicted, of course. Didn't they tell us we were going to have a few more days of warm weather before the cold set in?"

"I did hear something like…"

"They just never know, do they? Here, now, let me take your coat. And just leave your boots there. Finding your boots when you leave is something of a standard Christmas game, isn't it? Last year, I went home in someone else's." Her forehead furrowed. "They were men's size ten mukluks. I do wonder who ended up with my size sixes. I'm Mimi Saunders, by the way. Please just call me Mimi. Mrs. Saunders makes me feel quite old. Now you just come on in, and I'll see if I can find Hemp."

"No," Amanda said urgently. Mimi gave her a quizzical look and Amanda rushed on. "You see, Mrs. Saunders…uh, Mimi, I'm not Hemp's…"

"You're not Hemp's daughter?" Mimi peered into her face. "I must admit, I was wondering. You don't look at all like him or Margery, do you?"

"Probably not," Amanda agreed. "I…"

"Of course, you could always be the result of some wild fling." Mimi giggled and her face lit up with mirth. "But it's difficult to imagine Hemp having a wild fling—or anyone having a wild fling with Hemp.'' She turned as another woman wandered into the hall, this one slightly taller and more angularly built. ''Oh, here's Eeedee. Eeedee, this is...Amanda, isn't it? She's not Hemp's daughter.''

''Of course she isn't,'' Eeedee said briskly. ''Anyone looking at her can see that.'' She held out a hand. ''Hello, Amanda. Are you one of Charmaine's friends?''

''No,'' said Amanda, shaking hands. ''I'm...''

''Thank goodness for that.'' Eeedee leaned closer and lowered her voice. ''Not that there's anything wrong with Charmaine—or her friends. But they do tend to go and on about this cosmic connection thing. I think it's because most of them are from Detroit.''

''I've never been to Detroit,'' Amanda assured her. She looked curiously around the wide entranceway, admiring the pale green carpet and pastel walls. Not only were Josh's relatives not gargoyles but this one appeared to have good decorating sense.

''I've never been to Detroit, either,'' said Eeedee. ''I did spend a little time in Denver, though. I quite liked it there. I'm Edwina Davidson, by the way. Everyone calls me Eeedee. I don't really mind, although it does sound like they're reciting the alphabet backward.''

''Edwina,'' Amanda echoed. Then she made the connection. ''Edwina Davidson. You must be Josh's mother.''

''Why, yes, I...'' Edwina stopped talking and stared at Amanda out of two brown eyes that looked a lot like her son's. ''You know *Josh*?''

''Yes.'' Amanda felt herself flushing under Edwina's incredulous gaze. "He sort of...invited me here."

"Josh invited you here," Edwina repeated in a stunned-sounding voice. She turned to her stepsister. "Did you hear that, Mimi? Josh invited her here."

They both stared at Amanda as if she were the gargoyle. Amanda felt as if she'd made an enormous social blunder. "You see, he—I...that is...he asked me to..." She realized she was babbling and took a breath. "He said no one would mind."

"Mind?" Edwina beamed at her. "Of course we don't mind." She slipped her arm through Amanda's. "As a matter of fact, we're absolutely delighted."

"AND THESE ARE Josh's sisters," Edwina concluded. She gestured toward a group of three women, none of whom appeared to be "a lot older" than Josh. "This is Marilla, Shelby, and Charmaine. Darlings, this is Amanda." She paused for dramatic effect. "Josh's friend, Amanda."

There was a split second of silence that was broken by the women's excited chatter. "A girlfriend? Josh?"

"When did this all happen?" asked Shelby, her round, intelligent face alive with curiosity while the stunningly beautiful Charmaine shook Amanda's hand with outright enthusiasm. "I do hope you're considering a Christmas wedding. Christmas weddings are so...cosmic!"

"We're not considering any wedding," said Amanda. "As a matter of fact—"

"Honestly, Charmaine!" Marilla interrupted. "Can't you see things haven't got to that point yet? If you aren't careful, you'll scare her off." She gave

Charmaine a disgusted look and produced a friendly smile for Amanda. ''Don't worry about it, Amanda. Charmaine can find something cosmic in almost any date.''

''Every day is a cosmic day,'' Charmaine retorted, apparently not the least bit upset by her sister's attitude. ''Except the Ides of March. It has really bad connotations. I wouldn't get married on that date.''

Her smile was just as friendly as Marilla's. Amanda smiled back. Josh had misled her about his relatives, she decided. There wasn't anything wrong with them—except they all had a disturbing tendency to jump to conclusions. ''I'm not thinking about any date,'' she told Charmaine. ''But if I were, I wouldn't choose the Ides of March. Listen, I should explain…''

''Oh, please do,'' said Shelby. ''We're all agog with curiosity. How did you meet Josh?''

''I just walked into his office. I…''

''Ah,'' said Charmaine. ''Love at first sight.'' She dug an elbow into Marilla's side. ''Doesn't that sound like a cosmic connection?''

''Not really,'' said Marilla. ''It does sound romantic, though. What happened, Amanda? Did you just stare at each other and decide this was it?''

''I wouldn't exactly…''

''Amanda?'' called a male voice.

Amanda turned to see Josh maneuvering his way across the crowded room. He had on a pair of dark trousers, a white shirt, and a deep brown-and-green-patterned sweater that accented the hazel glints of his eyes. Amanda had never been so happy to see someone. That was just because she wanted him to clear up this misunderstanding, she told herself. It had nothing to do with how good he looked.

He stopped beside her and smiled down at her. "I didn't see you come in."

"I...uh...just got here," Amanda murmured, flustered by his nearness.

Josh glanced around the group. "I take it you've met my mother and my sisters?"

"Yes, I..."

"Yes, she has," Edwina interrupted. "And we're absolutely delighted, Josh." She gave him a little swat on the arm. "But you really should have told us sooner."

Josh's eyebrows gathered together, displaying his confusion. "Told you sooner about what?"

"About Amanda," explained Marilla. "Or, rather, you and Amanda."

"Me and Amanda," Josh echoed, his tone as blank as his expression.

"Why didn't you tell us?" asked Charmaine.

"Didn't you think we'd like her?" asked Marilla.

"Or did you want to surprise us?" asked Shelby.

Everyone looked at him expectantly. Josh's gaze met Amanda's, his expression still confused. Amanda cleared her throat. "I was just, um, trying to explain to your family about our...relationship."

"Ah. Our relationship."

"That's right." Amanda looked around the ensemble of faces. "You see, Josh and I aren't—"

"It's okay, darling," Josh interrupted. His eyes sparkled with merriment, his dimple flashed with his smile. He put an arm around Amanda and gave her a little hug. "They're my family. I want them to know." He smiled fondly into her eyes. His aunts, his mother and his stepsisters smiled fondly at them.

The only one who wasn't smiling was Amanda.

She was busy planning on the long, torturous method she was going to use to murder Josh Larkland.

"I PERSONALLY PREFER the short-haired varieties," Marilla explained earnestly. "Although I had an Angora once who was quite delightful." She raised an eyebrow in Amanda's direction. "What do you think?"

"I've, uh, actually never had much to do with cats," Amanda stuttered. "But...um, I do find them...intriguing."

"They certainly are. I just knew you'd feel that way," Marilla said, then gave Amanda a big smile. "Who knows? Maybe there is something to this cosmic connection stuff of Charmaine's."

Amanda couldn't do anything more than smile back. That was the worst part of all this. She liked these people—and they seemed to like her. The only person she didn't like was Josh. "Maybe there is," she said to Marilla. "Will you excuse me? I, uh, need to have a word with Josh."

Marilla nodded indulgently. "Ah, yes. Romance. Isn't it wonderful?"

"Just splendid," Amanda muttered. She maneuvered her way through the crowd to find Josh. He was standing with a couple of older men, cheerfully knocking back a glass of eggnog punch. "Ah, here she is now," he said as Amanda came up. He rested a casual arm across her shoulders. "Darling. Have you met Uncle Frank and Aunt Louise? Uncle Frank is an investment counselor."

"That's right," said Frank. He shook Amanda's hand enthusiastically. "Frank Bromwell. It's a pleasure to meet you. I was just telling Josh that he should get together with me in the New Year. Now that you're thinking of settling down, you should also be thinking about retirement.''

"What a splendid idea," Amanda enthused before Josh could say anything. "You really should do that, honey. It sounds fascinating." She slipped her hand through Josh's arm. "Will you excuse us, please? I need to have a word with Josh."

"You two go right ahead." Louise gave them a misty look. "We remember how it is, don't we, Frank?" They wandered off, arm in arm.

As soon as they were out of earshot, Josh turned to Amanda. "Well?" he whispered. "How are you doing? Have you found out anything personal about them yet?"

"Only that Marilla likes cats. Josh, we have to do something about this. These people…"

Josh shook his head. "We can't do anything about them, Amanda. They've always been like this."

"Well, I haven't always been like this. Josh, they think you and I are…are…romantically involved."

"Do they?" he asked, and he took another sip of his drink. "I wonder why."

Amanda narrowed her eyes. "You know very well why they think that!"

Josh made a futile attempt to look philosophical. "I seldom know why they think anything."

"Well, in this case, I believe it's obvious. *You*…"

Josh put a finger over her lips. "Shh. Someone will hear you."

"I want them to hear me. I…"

"Shh!" Josh said again. He took her hand and led her through the dining room and into the kitchen.

"Now, what's the problem?" he asked as soon as they were alone.

Amanda withdrew her hand and backed into a white kitchen counter. "What do you think the problem is?" she snapped. "The problem is that these people think we are...involved." Her voice rose. "And they think that because *you* told them..."

Josh shrugged. "I had to tell them something." She frowned and he sighed. "Well, what was I supposed to say? I couldn't very well tell them that you're my Christmas elf, now could I?"

"There's a big difference between elf and...and what those people are thinking."

"Not really." He put a hand on one shoulder and guided her further into the kitchen. "Your flyer did say that you'd provide everything I need to have a Merry Christmas."

Amanda was starting to heartily regret that flyer. "Yes, but..."

"Well, right now it looks like I need a girlfriend. Otherwise they'll force one on me."

"Then maybe you should find a real one!" Amanda flung.

"What? Between now and five minutes from now?" Josh shook his head. "Not only is that impossible, but I don't want to do it. Besides, this is your big chance to find out something personal about all these people. Did you see how they reacted out there? They're all dying to meet you...to talk to you."

"Yes, but..."

"So you shouldn't have any problem finding out something personal about them." He grinned triumphantly.

At that very second Amanda could have cheerfully throttled him. "It's not as if they just think we're dating, Josh! They think we're...we're serious."

"So?"

"So, it isn't true."

He shrugged. "They don't need to know that."

Amanda gaped at him. "Josh Larkland, that is the worst thing I've ever heard anyone say. You can't go around lying to your relatives...especially at Christmas."

"I didn't lie! They just jumped to a conclusion, that's all."

"A conclusion you did nothing to correct."

"No, I didn't," Josh said. "And I'm not going to, either." He gestured toward the living room. "You saw what it's like out there. They've got women lined up wall-to-wall to meet me."

Amanda thought of the three predatory women she'd been introduced to. "Some of them could be very nice," she said, lying through her teeth.

"Ha!"

"Josh!"

"Oh, come on, Amanda. I don't have anything to say to the owner of a dress shop, a cat groomer, or someone trying to cast cosmic spells!"

Amanda wrinkled her nose. "They are a little...eccentric I suppose. But that's still no reason..."

"It's a very good reason! If I wasn't here with you, they'd all pounce on me. Then they'd phone, asking when we could get together. Marilla, Charmaine, Mimi, my mother, and God knows who else would call me, asking me when I'm going to see them again. I'd have to think up some excuse, or else spend a lot of time seeing women I'm not the least bit interested in seeing. This way, I don't have to do that." He shrugged.

"Yes, but..."

"And as for my relatives, well, it pretty much serves them right! They're the ones who leapt to the wrong conclusion."

"They had a very good reason to leap to the wrong conclusion. You—"

Josh held up a hand. "Okay. Maybe I did give them a little nudge. But they were all ready to do it. And it's not as if we're hurting anyone. They're happy! And they all seem to like you."

They did, too. As a matter of fact, Amanda couldn't remember the last time she'd been in a room where everyone thought she was the most marvelous human being on the face of the earth. "Yes, they're happy now. But how happy will they be when they find out the truth?"

Josh looked baffled. "How would they find that out? I'm not going to tell them."

Could he possibly be this dense? "You'll have to tell them something," Amanda explained very slowly. "The next time you come to one of these things..."

Josh shrugged that off. "I have no intention of coming to another one of these things anytime in the near future. That's part of your job, remember? You are going to come up with reasons why I can't."

"But..."

"And if they ask, I'll just say I'm not seeing you anymore. That won't be a lie."

"No, it wouldn't, but..."

Josh sighed and leaned against the kitchen cabinet next to her. "Oh, come on, Amanda, don't make a

big deal out of this. It's just one evening. All you
have to do is exactly what you're doing. And it's a
perfect opportunity for you to find out personal stuff
about all these people.''

It almost made sense, in a weird, illogical sort of
way. Almost.

"Besides, what else can you do?" Josh asked.
"You'll never convince those people you aren't involved with me. They *want* to believe it.''

"Well, uh…"

"And who knows," Josh added, "it might be kind
of fun.''

"In what way?''

He stroked a finger down her cheek, making her
shiver. "Lots of ways.''

Amanda stepped away. "You were a really bad
child, weren't you?''

"The very worst," he said solemnly.

Mimi's booming voice could be heard coming from
the living room. "They're in the kitchen, Edwina.
And I think they're kissing!''

"There, see," said Josh. "You really don't have
any choice, do you?''

"THAT WAS MORE FUN than I've had at one of those
things in decades," Josh announced as they climbed
into his car a few hours later.

He sprawled back in the seat, one of his arms
stretched along the back, his right thigh just touching
hers. "As soon as everyone saw you, they pretty
much left me alone." He glanced over at her, grinning. "I should have gotten an elf years ago." He
started the car and pulled out into traffic.

"You should have gotten a girlfriend years ago,"

Amanda scolded. "Haven't you ever introduced a date to your family before?"

Josh considered it, then shook his head. "I don't think so. At least, not recently."

"Why not?" She glanced sideways at him. "You do have dates, don't you?"

"Of course I have dates," said Josh, sounding a little defensive about it. "But I don't take them home to meet my family the first time we go out."

Amanda thought about the way she'd been received. "That's probably a good idea," she agreed. "However, after you've been together a couple of months, you could do it. Or don't you date the same person that long?"

"Well, not usually, no."

"Why not?" Amanda asked, still looking at him.

"I don't know." He was starting to sound really defensive now. "I just get busy and...and don't." He angled his head so he could see her. "What about you? Do you date a lot?"

Amanda thought about the last couple of men she'd been involved with. They hadn't really "dated." She'd spent more time cleaning Dwight's apartment than they had going anywhere. She had been out with Kyle quite often—but that was just to a doughnut shop. He'd fed her endless cups of coffee while he'd told her about his problems. "Off and on," she muttered.

"And do you introduce these 'on and off' dates to your family?"

"I would," said Amanda. "But my family doesn't live anywhere around here."

"Where do they live, then? The North Pole?"

"No," said Amanda. "My parents live in Yellow-knife."

"Yellowknife? As in the Northwest Territories?" Josh snorted. "That's close enough to the North Pole for me."

"Sometimes it does feel like the North Pole," Amanda admitted. "It's so far away. I don't get back there to visit as often as I'd like." Amanda would love to have family like his around. But her relatives were scattered all over the country. Her parents were up north. Her brother was down east and her sister was in the States. They kept in touch with phone calls but it wasn't the same as living in the same city. It seemed rather ironic. She'd enjoy being closer to her family, and Josh seemed to wish he didn't have a family.

Josh patted her arm. "You can always hitch a ride on Santa's sleigh. I'm sure he wouldn't mind an elf perched among the toys. And speaking of elves, how did your elf business go tonight? Did you find out a whole lot of personal stuff about people?"

"Not a lot." Amanda leaned back and closed her eyes. "They all wanted to talk about me. Or you."

"Me?" Josh sounded alarmed. "What did they say about me?"

"Only that you spend too much time in your office and not enough time with them."

"Oh." He chuckled. "They're always saying stuff like that. I don't know why. I spend lot of time with them."

"Sure you do," Amanda said dryly. "That's why you know so many personal things about them."

"I found out something," Josh objected. "I now know that Uncle Frank is an investment counselor."

"How insightful," Amanda muttered.

"Hey, you spent a whole evening with them and the only thing you seemed to have found out is that they don't think I spend enough time with them. That doesn't sound very personal to me."

"It's hard to find out personal things about that many people in one evening," Amanda retorted. "They're your relatives. If anyone should be finding out personal things about them it should be you." She paused. "Besides, I did find out something. Your aunt Mimi collects Halsone's."

"Halsone's? What are those?"

"You can't have missed them, Josh. They're all over the house. Those little rabbit ornaments."

"Oh, those." He blinked. "Are they personal?"

"If you collect them, they are. Personal...and expensive."

"How do you know these things?"

"They're in all the stores." She considered it. "I didn't see the clown one there. That might be a good one to get her."

"Good," said Josh. "One down. What about the others?"

"I'll...give it some thought." Now that she had a face to connect with names, it should be a little easier.

Josh parked the car in the loading zone in front of her apartment building, and walked her to her door. Amanda took the key out of her pocket and turned to face Josh. "Well, good night. Thanks for taking me. I enjoyed it."

"So did I," said Josh.

"I just hope they aren't going to be too upset when they find out I'm not your girlfriend."

"But you were," said Josh. "At least for tonight,

anyway.'' He put his hands on her shoulders, turning her to face him. ''And since you are, it seems to me...''

He was going to kiss her. Amanda realized it as his head started to descend. She could easily have stopped it. She could have moved away, or pushed him away.

But she didn't. She stood very still as he touched his lips to hers, lightly, then deeply. A soft, unthreatening kiss, filled with charm and warmth, while one of his fingers brushed down her cheek and his tongue stroked her lips. When he moved away, she was hot and shaky and gasping for breath. ''Good night, Amanda,'' he said, and then he was gone.

Amanda watched the door close after him. A business relationship, she reminded herself. That's all this was.

She was going to have to concentrate hard on keeping it that way.

4

"YOU'RE IN A GOOD MOOD this morning," Mable accused.

She set a stack of technical manuals on Josh's desk, and studied him with a mixture of suspicion and astonishment. "You haven't yelled at me once, you even said thank-you, and just now I thought I heard you whistling 'Santa Claus is Coming to Town.' What's going on?"

"Nothing is going on," said Josh. He chose one of the manuals from the stack and began flipping through it.

"Oh." Mable's suspicious look increased in intensity. "In that case, I can only conclude that your body has been taken over by aliens."

Josh chuckled. "My body hasn't been taken over by anything. I'm just in a good mood. After all, it is Christmas. People are supposed to be in a good mood around Christmas."

"You aren't," said Mable. "Christmas brings out the worst in you. Why, just yesterday you were trying to get me to reschedule it...or buy you a ticket to January."

"Or find me a Christmas elf," Josh reminded her. "Since you did that, you don't have to do any of those other things."

"A Christmas elf?" For a second Mable looked

blank. Then she smiled. "Ah, yes. The woman from that executive services company. The one who's doing the Christmas party for us."

"Uh-huh," said Josh. "Along with other things."

"Other things? What other things?" Her eyes widened. "Oh, no. Don't tell me you talked that poor young woman into doing your Christmas shopping for you?"

"She's…helping me with it." Josh saw the look of disapproval on Mable's face and winced. "Is there something wrong with that?"

"Of course there's something wrong with it! Your mother didn't ask you to get personal presents for people just so you could slough it off on a stranger!"

Josh felt a pang of guilt, which he immediately suppressed. "I didn't have any choice. You wouldn't do it, and I don't have time." He bent his head to avoid seeing the censure in Mable's eyes. "Besides, Amanda isn't a stranger. She met everybody last night."

"Last night?"

"That's right," said Josh. "I took her to Mimi's party."

"You went to Mimi's party?" Mable's eyes widened. "I thought you didn't go to family gatherings of more than four people."

"I don't," said Josh. "But I had to go to that one so Amanda could meet everybody and find out personal stuff about them."

"Oh, for heaven's sake, Josh!" Mable exclaimed. She put her hands on her hips and positively glared at him. "That is the tackiest thing I've ever heard of. They are *your* relatives, you know. If anyone is going to find out personal things about them, it should be you!''

Josh winced. ''Yeah, well, Amanda mentioned something like that herself.''

''Did she?'' said Mable.

''Yeah.'' Josh mulled it over, then shoved the small concern aside. ''But I'm sure she'll manage.''

''I think she just might,'' said Mable. She smiled. ''You know, I think I'm going to like Amanda.''

''Of course you'll like her. Everyone likes an elf.'' Josh looked up. ''But don't go spreading it around that that's what she is. I don't want anybody to know that I've got an elf.''

''You don't have to worry about that,'' Mable muttered. ''That's one secret that's safe with me.'' She walked out, shaking her head.

Josh watched her leave, then switched on his computer. This was working out wonderfully. His Christmas problems were solved. He could forget all about it and get back to concentrating on work.

''JUST A MINUTE,'' said Brandy. ''I'll see if she's in.'' She put a hand over the receiver and raised an eyebrow in Amanda's direction. ''It's someone named Charmaine,'' she announced in a stage whisper. Amanda shook her head. Brandy sighed and put the receiver to her ear again. ''I'm sorry, Charmaine, she can't come to phone right now. Yes…yes, I'll tell her you called.'' She hung up the phone and turned around. ''That was Charmaine,'' she said unnecessarily. ''Let me guess. She's related to Josh Larkland.''

''Uh-huh,'' said Amanda.

''I figured as much.'' Brandy dropped into a

kitchen chair. "At least it wasn't Harvy Denton again. He's called three times this morning to apologize. I'm starting to think he really is sorry."

"Maybe he is," said Amanda. "He did send you flowers. And didn't he say he got the wrong impression yesterday?"

"Uh-huh. He said he thought I was gorgeous and when I sat down and asked him how I could make his Christmas merrier, he thought I was making a pass at him."

Amanda pictured the sultry-looking Brandy saying those words. "It is possible that…"

"Maybe it is," Brandy interrupted. "But that still doesn't make it right. He should have *asked* before he lunged." She folded her arms. "I told him that, too."

"Oh? And what did he say?"

"He agreed with me." Brandy's lips twitched into a smile. "But he explained it by saying that he hadn't had much experience dating since his divorce and that he thought that might be the way it was done these days. Can you imagine?"

Amanda was starting to feel a little sorry for Harvy Denton. "Well," she said. "I suppose it is possible…."

"I suppose," said Brandy. "Now he wants me to come back to the office and give him another chance. I've told him no three times, but he just isn't getting the message."

"Maybe you should give him another chance," Amanda said tentatively. "Maybe he is a nice guy. If you want, we could go together and…"

"I've had enough wrestling matches for one month. Forget it, Amanda. I don't want to have anything to do with Harvy. He's a creep. Once a creep, always a creep.''

"You never know,'' said Amanda. Her mind reverted to their most recent phone call. "What did Charmaine say?''

"The same thing as everyone else…she wants to get together with you.'' Brandy gave her a curious look. "These relatives of Josh Larkland's have been calling you all morning. So far we've had Judith, who wants to have tea with you. Shelby, who wanted to make sure you'd come to her party. And now Charmaine, who wanted you to go to some sort of cosmetology class.''

"Not cosmetology,'' Amanda corrected. "Cosmicology.''

"What's that?''

"It has something to do with being connected with the galaxy.'' She leaned back in the kitchen chair. "It's too bad I can't get together with Charmaine. It might be interesting.'' She wouldn't mind having tea with Aunt Judith, either, or going to Shelby's.

"So why don't you?''

"I can't, Brandy. The only reason these people want to get together with me is because they think I'm Josh's girlfriend. And I'm not.'' She frowned down at her list on the table, wishing that the business would really take off so they could start working out of an office, and finally get out of her kitchen.

Brandy ran her fingers through her hair. "We've had more phone calls this morning than we've had since we started this business. If they were about business, I'd be ecstatic. But they aren't. They're either Mr. Denton for me, or a bunch of Josh's relatives for you.'' She put her head to one side and stared at

Amanda. "What did you do to those people anyway?"

"I didn't do anything except walk into a room." Amanda picked up a cup of coffee from the table. As she drank it, she studied the list of Josh's relatives in front of her. "It was remarkable, Brandy. I have never been so socially accepted in my entire life. Everyone wanted to talk to me. It was almost like being back home."

"I don't suppose they wanted to talk about arranging some sort of business party?" Brandy said dryly.

"I'm afraid not." Amanda studied the list, then sighed loudly. "Unfortunately, they didn't want to talk about Christmas presents, either. All they wanted to talk about was me...or Josh."

"All you want to talk about is Josh," Brandy complained. "Since I've got here you've said his name about three hundred times."

"No, I haven't," Amanda objected, although she knew it wasn't true. Her mind did keep drifting off into happy little tangents about the sparkle in Josh's eyes, the feel of his cheek brushing against hers, the warmth of his lips... Amanda gave her head a slight shake. "I'm just trying to come up with suitable presents for these people."

"It's more than that," Brandy said disapprovingly as she leaned forward. "You're falling for Josh Larkland, aren't you?"

"No, I'm not," Amanda said firmly. "He is a sweet guy, though, Brandy. Charming when he wants to be. Good-looking." And a great kisser, too. She didn't think Brandy needed to know about that. "And he has a really nice family."

"Who he doesn't care about one little bit," Brandy reminded her.

"I'm not sure that's true," Amanda objected. "I think he cares about them. He did spend most of the evening asking them how old they were and what they did for a living."

"Something he already should have known," Brandy noted, sounding less than impressed.

"And he gets tired of them always criticizing him," Amanda said, ignoring her. "They're always trying to line him up with someone. You should have seen the women they produced at Mimi's. I don't think they realize that some men just don't want to be lined up. As a matter of fact, I don't think they understand him at all."

"That makes two of us," Brandy muttered. "Or, in his case, twenty-two of us."

"He's not that difficult to understand. He's just one of those people who's totally wrapped up in his work." Amanda stared off into space again. "It's a simple lack of communication. He doesn't communicate with his family and they don't communicate with him. If they got together more often..."

"Don't do it, Amanda," Brandy warned.

"Don't do what?" Amanda said, looking up with an innocent expression.

"Get involved in this. You're an executive services person, not a family therapist."

"I know," Amanda said softly. "But it *is* Christmas."

"You can't reform people, even at Christmas. You certainly can't reform men. It's like getting something on sale. What you see is what you get—missing buttons and all."

"I'm not..."

"You're thinking about it. We've both done this before. We date a guy whose an obvious loser, with the hopes of changing him. It never works. *Never.*" She raised an eyebrow. "Remember Kyle? You paid for all the dates, and spent hours listening to his problems. Then he dumped you and went off with some bimbo cocktail waitress from Vancouver."

"Actually she was from Victoria. And..."

"Then there was Dwight," Brandy said, warming to the topic. "You lent him money, helped him get a job, and as soon as he got a few bucks together, he announced he wasn't ready for any sort of commitment."

Amanda shifted in the chair, her face heating up. "All right," she said. "Maybe I do have lousy taste in men. But this time it's different."

"Yeah right! Not only are you getting involved with Josh Larkland, you're also getting involved with his entire extended family!"

"I'm not getting involved with any of them," Amanda said in an unconvincing tone.

Brandy threw up her hands. "That's not how it sounds," she said, sounding skeptical.

"Well, that's how it is. I doubt I'll see his family again—unless I happen to run into them on the street." Which she fervently hoped wouldn't happen. She couldn't imagine what she'd say to them. "And I won't be seeing Josh again, either," she added.

"You won't?"

"No, I won't. At least, not the way you mean. Oh, I'll probably run into him a few times while I'm organizing his office party, although I suspect I'll be spending more time with his secretary than I will with him.''

Brandy didn't look persuaded. Not one bit. ''You're sure of that?''

''Absolutely positive.'' She was, too. In spite of the wonderful evening and terrific kiss, she knew very well that Josh wasn't interested in her. She was his Christmas elf, that's all—the person who was going to solve all his Christmas problems. She doubted he even remembered her name this morning.

IN TRUTH, Josh wasn't having any problems remembering Amanda's name—or a lot of other things about her.

She'd drifted across his mind more than once this morning—odd thought fragments about the silky feel of her blond hair, the way she'd looked in that red dress, and the tantalizing touch of her mouth against his. Memories of Amanda kept disturbing his concentration. So far this morning he had gotten nowhere on the network interface he was supposed to be redesigning.

And if he hadn't had his own unruly memories to remind him about Amanda, there was always his family.

A number of them had called this morning to wax enthusiastically about her. ''She's absolutely delightful, Josh.'' ''Such a charming girl, Josh.'' And, from his Aunt Judith, for some obscure reason, ''She's so intriguing, Josh. I understand she has a green bathroom.'' It seemed everyone approved of her—and wanted to see her again.

At first Josh had enjoyed their approval. However, when his mother called, he started to feel a tiny bit guilty. So when Edwina said, "I must say, there have been times when I wasn't sure if you were going to settle down—or what kind of girl you'd settle down with. It's such a relief to know that you've found someone like Amanda," he tried to tone things down. "We aren't exactly settled down, Mom."

"I know, dear," Edwina said in a wise-sounding voice. "But you are going to keep on seeing her, aren't you?"

"Of course I'm going to keep on seeing her," Josh muttered. Come to think of it, though, he didn't know *when* he'd see Amanda again. She'd be off doing elf-type stuff and he'd be working.

He gave his head a slight shake. Of course he was going to see her again. She was his elf. Apart from that, there was that kiss to consider. His mind reverted to the soft, luscious feel of her lips, only to be dragged back by Edwina's cheerful "In that case, I think I should get to know her better."

"Do you?" Josh was still enjoying the warm rush he was experiencing remembering Amanda's kiss.

"Yes. I'd like to have lunch with her sometime."

"Sure," Josh muttered absently.

"How about today?"

"Today?" Josh straightened in his chair. "I don't know about today."

"Then how about tomorrow?"

"I'm…uh…not sure," Josh mumbled. "I'll have to check with Amanda."

"Could you do that, dear? I've been trying to get her all morning but she wasn't available. Maybe when you're talking to her…"

Josh was almost positive he knew what Amanda's reaction would be, but before he could think of a way to put his mother off, she'd said goodbye and hung up.

Josh had just replaced the receiver when Mable buzzed through on the intercom. "Hank Turnbull on line one," she reported.

Josh studied the blinking light, then picked up the phone. "Hi, Hank. What's up?"

Hank's baritone, smooth and rich, eased out of the receiver. "To be perfectly honest, I'm calling to check out the gossip."

"Gossip?" Josh echoed. "What gossip?"

"About you." Hank chuckled. "I understand there's a new woman in your life."

Josh gave the phone a quizzical look. He'd been dealing with Hank for over a year now. Apart from mentioning his wife and kids, and once having to leave a meeting early to attend his son's hockey game, Hank had never made a personal remark about himself, or Josh. "Oh?" Josh said slowly. "How did you hear that?"

"Well…" Hank chuckled again. "Ed Baigly was talking to Jon Fieldman, who knows your uncle Reginald. He mentioned you brought a woman home to meet the family last night."

Josh had no idea why Hank would be interested in something as far away from business as this. "Uhhuh."

"So it's true, then?"

"Yeah, it's true." Josh was intrigued by Hank's interest. "Why are you…"

"It's not just idle curiosity," Hank assured him. "It's business."

Josh struggled to understand what Hank was talking about. "Business?"

"That's right. This might be exactly what we need to push some of those potential investors into current investors."

"Huh?"

"It's a question of reliability," Hank explained. "Everyone knows you're brilliant, but it's the other things that make people nervous. A married man does seem less risky. More solid. More mature."

"A married man?" Josh repeated, startled. "I'm not…"

"No, I know you're not, but from the way Reg was talking it sounds as if that's just around the corner." Hank chuckled. "Is she going to be at your office Christmas party?"

"I expect so, but…"

"Excellent. Excellent. Be sure to introduce her around. Oh, and why don't you bring her to our open house next week? Rhonda and I would like to meet her."

"I'll…uh…have to check with Amanda," Josh improvised. "I'm not sure of our schedule."

He hung up the phone and tapped his fingers thoughtfully on his desk. His Christmas elf was turning out to be more helpful—and more necessary—than he'd originally planned.

IT WAS JUST BEFORE ELEVEN when Josh phoned. Brandy was out trying to drum up more business so Amanda was forced to answer the phone. "People have been trying to get you all morning," he complained when Amanda said a tentative hello. "Where have you been?"

Amanda lost herself in the sound of his voice. She

could picture him sitting in his office, with papers strewn all over his desk. "In and out."

"Shopping?" he asked eagerly.

Of course. That's why he was calling. "I'm working on it," Amanda said.

"Good. Listen, are you free for lunch?"

Amanda's spirits rose. "Why, yes, I am."

"Great. My mother wants to have lunch with you."

Amanda bounced from dreamland back into reality. "Your mother?"

"Uh-huh. She wants to get to know you better."

"Wonderful," Amanda said sarcastically. This was some switch. Usually it was the mother who didn't like the girlfriend. This time, it was only the mother who liked the girlfriend—and she wasn't really a girlfriend. "I don't think that's a good idea."

"You don't?" Josh sounded as clued out as usual. "Why not?"

Honestly! "Because I don't." Amanda tapped her foot with irritation. "I told you last night that I didn't want to keep misleading your family."

"You also told me last night that you didn't find out a whole lot of personal things about everyone."

"True, but..."

"This would be a great opportunity to find out more. You could quiz my mother. I'm sure she knows a lot of personal stuff about people."

There were still a lot of question marks on her gift list. Edwina would undoubtedly be an excellent source of information. "I suppose it would, but..."

"Then why don't we have lunch with her and find out something?"

"I really don't..." Amanda paused. "Are you coming, too?"

"Sure. I can give you a hand with the personal stuff. Besides, there's something I need to discuss with you."

Amanda started to refuse again, then reconsidered. From what she'd heard last night, she'd say it had been a long time since Josh had lunched with his mother—or done anything else with her. Edwina would be so pleased if he did. It *would* give Amanda a chance to find out more about Josh's relatives—maybe enable her to fill in a few blanks on her Christmas shopping list.

And besides, she wouldn't mind seeing him again, either.

"All right," she said. "I suppose…"

"Good," said Josh. "Twelve o'clock at Charbais. And don't be late. Mom hates it when people are late."

Amanda hung up the phone and smiled. At least that was *one* thing Josh knew about his mother.

IT WAS TWO MINUTES PAST twelve when Amanda walked into Charbais. Edwina was already seated. Josh was nowhere in sight.

He'd better make an appearance, Amanda thought as she followed the maître d' to the table. Getting Josh together with his mother was the main reason she'd accepted this invitation. She also intended to find out as much as she could about Edwina as well as the other members of the family. Then she could erase all the question marks on her gift list. Furthermore, she was determined to convince Edwina that her relationship with Josh was extremely casual.

Actually, convincing Edwina probably wouldn't be the difficult part. The difficult part was that Amanda couldn't bring herself to do it. Edwina was so...delighted. Amanda realized that about six seconds after she was seated in the elegant upscale restaurant. "I'm so pleased you could come," Edwina said as the maître d' handed Amanda a menu. "I want to get to know you better." She reached across the table to squeeze Amanda's hand. "I want us to be friends."

Amanda doubted Josh's mother would feel that way if she knew the truth. "I'd like that, too," she said. She took a long swallow of water. "But I really should explain that Josh and I...that is, our relationship is very, uh, casual."

"Oh, dear," Edwina said faintly. She took a sip from her water glass. "I was afraid you were going to say something like that."

Amanda gaped at her. "You were?"

"Yes." Her lips turned down at the corners. "It's us, isn't it? We scared you off last night."

She looked so despondent that Amanda rushed to reassure her. "Oh, no. You were all wonderful. It's just that..."

"I know, dear." Edwina stretched forward to pat her hand. "You have to understand, Amanda. We've all been so concerned about Josh. We don't see much of him. He buries himself in his office and doesn't come out for weeks at a time. And he really doesn't have much of a life—or if he does, he doesn't share it with us."

"I do understand, but..."

"I blame myself, you know. After all, I did marry a man with three daughters. Not that there's anything wrong with them." Her forehead creased. "Charmaine can be a bit odd at times, and Marilla can be excessive about her cats. But Shelby is a darling. And they all mean well.''

''Of course they do,'' Amanda assured her. ''I liked all of them. And I'm sure your marriage…''

''It might have,'' said Edwina, sighing. ''Josh was seven when I remarried. The girls are much older and…well, they spoiled him. So did Mimi and Louise. They're Harold's sisters. Unfortunately, neither of them have children so they lavished all their attention on Josh. It was easy to do, even then. He's an easy person to like, don't you think?''

''He certainly is.''

''He's also a little self-centered, and he's much too fond of getting his own way. That's partly because he's very clever, and party because of us.''

''I don't think…''

''Yes, he is. But he can also be amazingly thoughtful, and exceedingly generous, when he gets around to thinking about it. The trouble is, he doesn't think about it very much anymore.'' She smiled sadly. ''Now that you're part of his life, I hope he'll think about it more often. And maybe we'll see a little more of him, too.''

Amanda would have loved to be able to tell this sweet woman that this was going to happen. Unfortunately, that wasn't the case. She took a deep breath. ''I'm not really part—'' She started.

What she was trying to say was interrupted by a commotion at the entrance. Amanda looked up to see Josh striding through the restaurant. He had on a pair of black jeans, his hair had obviously been combed by a hand, his running shoes were covered in snow, and every woman in the place was staring at him.

He stopped beside their table, and bent to kiss his mother on the cheek. "Hi, Mom. Sorry I'm late."

Edwina gaped at him. "I didn't realize you were joining us."

"You didn't?" He settled into a chair beside Amanda and smiled into her eyes. "Didn't Amanda tell you?"

Edwina shot Amanda a quizzical look. "She didn't mention it."

"It must have slipped her mind." He took Amanda's hand and slid his fingers through hers. "She left so early this morning I didn't have much of a chance to talk to her."

"She left early?" Edwina looked from one to the other. "You two are...living together?"

Amanda was still recovering from the sensation of his fingers closing around hers. "What?" she said. "Oh, no. No, we're...that is, I have my own place. I..."

"Yes, she does," Josh interrupted. "She just doesn't seem to spend a lot of time there."

"Ah," said Edwina. "I see."

"No, you don't," Amanda said desperately. "It's not like that. I..."

"That's okay, dear," Edwina soothed. "I understand completely...and I'm not at all prudish." She beamed at both of them, emanating happiness and approval. Josh looked smug.

Amanda sighed and gave up.

5

"THAT WAS WONDERFUL," Edwina said as they left the restaurant. She turned to Amanda. "Thanks so much for coming, Amanda, dear. I hope I'll be seeing a lot more of you."

I wouldn't count on it, Amanda thought. She'd hardly heard a word that had been spoken at lunch, being too preoccupied trying to find a way out of the situation she'd found herself in. She'd even considered telling Edwina the truth, but couldn't bring herself to do it. It might be what Josh deserved, but it wasn't what Edwina deserved. She'd be very hurt. No matter how annoyed Amanda was with Josh, she didn't want to upset Edwina.

She didn't feel that way about Josh, though. The second they were alone, she planned on telling him what an utter jerk she thought he was. She was also going to tell him what he could do with his job. He could figure out what to tell his relations. He winced at that. He was quite capable of telling them Amanda had been bumped off in a plane crash or had accepted a job in Siberia.

Outside the restaurant, Edwina gave Josh an extra-long hug. "I can't remember the last time we had lunch together. We really should do it more often." Then she affectionately patted his cheek. "And I hope you fixed that stove of yours for Amanda. It seems to

me the last time I was there you had to do something
with the television to get the burners to come on.''

As Edwina walked away Amanda stared after her,
then turned on Josh. ''All right, Josh Larkland, what
was that all about?''

''Hmm?'' He glanced down at her. ''Actually it
was about the microwave.''

''What?''

Josh put a hand on her back to guide her down the
busy street. ''You had to talk to the microwave to
turn on the television. It was a simple problem...and
I fixed it months ago.''

''I wasn't talking about that. I was talking about
what happened at lunch.''

''Lunch?'' Josh looked as if he'd forgotten he'd
eaten it. ''Oh, yeah, lunch. How was it? Did you find
out anything personal about...anyone?''

''Only about myself,'' Amanda complained. ''Just
out of idle curiosity, how did we go from casual
friends to living together in a little under twenty-four
hours?''

Josh stopped beside a bell-ringing Santa Claus and
dropped a handful of change into the collection box.
''I'm a fast worker when I make up my mind.'' He
shoved his hands into his pockets, pulled out a couple
of bills and dropped them in, as well, before starting
down the street. ''I think I fixed that problem with
the microwave sometime in the spring.''

''Good for you. Look, I...''

''Do you really think it's been that long since my
mother was over at my place?''

''No. Maybe you should have her over a little more
often.''

"That's a good idea," Josh said. "Why don't you arrange it?"

The suggestion caught Amanda off guard. Why didn't she arrange it? Maybe they could have more than his mother over. Maybe they could have his whole family. His family would certainly appreciate it. Of course Amanda had no idea how he lived. He probably had a downtown apartment ten seconds from his office, filled with ugly furniture and a truckload of high-tech equipment. It might not be a good place to entertain his family. On the other hand, they were his family. They had a right to know how he lived...

And that it wasn't with her. Amanda stopped walking and turned to face Josh. "Me? What do you mean, me?"

Josh stopped beside her and stared down at her with mild surprise. "You did say dinner parties were your specialty."

"*Business* dinner parties are my specialty," Amanda said from between clenched teeth.

"What's the difference? People eat and drink whether you work with them or are related to them."

"Yes, but..." Amanda gave her head a slight shake. She had to watch herself around this guy. He could use his weird logic to talk her into almost anything. "That is not the point! The point is that we can't go around deceiving people about our relationship."

"Why not?" he said nonchalantly. "You were perfectly willing to do it last night."

"I was not *willing* to do it last night! *You* talked me into it." Amanda realized she was raising her voice and lowered it a notch. "Besides, that was only supposed to be for one night. Now your mother thinks we're living together!''

''Yeah, well…uh.'' Josh cleared his throat. ''She's not the only one who thinks that.''

Amanda wasn't sure what he meant but she was positive she wasn't going to like it. ''She isn't?''

''No.'' Josh took a deep breath. ''Hank Turnbull called this morning. He's the guy who's lining up investors for me.''

''Oh?'' Amanda stared at him. ''Oh, no. Don't tell me you told him that we were living together, too?''

''Not exactly.'' Josh looked uncomfortable. ''He heard about us from Uncle Reggie.''

''Wonderful,'' Amanda muttered. She had a brief flash of all the people who'd been at Mimi's last night. If every one of them told a friend… ''Now the whole city thinks we're a couple.''

Josh gave her a bracing pat on the shoulder. ''Don't worry. They're all thrilled about it.''

''I'm not,'' Amanda muttered.

''Well, Hank is. It seems as if these investors aren't going to invest unless they think I'm mature and stable. Hank thinks I need some sort of…relationship to convince them of that.'' Josh looked as flummoxed by this as he did by everything else.

''I see,'' said Amanda. She had a strong suspicion she knew where this was leading. ''And I suppose you want me to pretend we have this…relationship.''

''Uh-huh,'' he said, nodding his head.

Amanda glanced up and down the street at the people hurrying by. ''Have you ever considered having a *real* relationship?''

''No,'' Josh admitted. ''But I would have if I'd known it was important.''

The helpless look in his brown eyes was enough to make the snow melt, much less Amanda's soft heart. Then he spoiled it by adding, "Besides, now I don't have to. I've got you."

"But…"

"It's too late to back out now, Amanda. My family thinks you're it, and apparently so does everyone else."

Amanda slumped back against the building. "Oh, no."

"What's wrong?" His eyes widened. "There isn't some guy hanging around you who is going to get mad about this, is there?"

"Well…no, but…"

"Good." He smiled in satisfaction. "I don't want some bozo in a leather jacket punching my face in."

"How about if a woman in a business suit does it?" Amanda asked, feeling very close to doing just that.

Josh chuckled. "I think I can handle an elf. Look, I'm not asking you to do anything unreasonable. I mean, you don't have to move in with me or anything."

"Good," said Amanda. "Because I wasn't planning on it. I am not going to do this, Josh. Deceiving your family for one night was bad enough. I…"

"It's for a good cause, Amanda."

"What cause? Getting your family off your back?" She shook her head. "I don't think…"

Josh took her arm. "Come on," he said. "There's something I want to show you."

AMANDA HAD BEEN in a number of high-tech offices but she'd never seen one quite like the room Josh had just ushered her into.

It was an enormous room, with wall-to-wall gray carpeting that went a foot up the side of the white walls. The ceiling was a continuous series of undulating ripples, and the walls were cut to match. The shelves at the back were filled with electronic equipment with hundreds of little blinking lights like an enormous, flat, wall-to-wall Christmas tree. The long counter was covered with computers, screens and stacks of paper.

The perimeter of the room was composed of six glassed-in compartments, each containing a desk, one or two computers, screens and equipment. All but one of these areas was occupied by one or two cleverlooking individuals, some engaged in animated conversation. However, the place where Amanda was standing was so quiet and so still she could have heard a pin drop. "What on earth…" she said.

"They're soundproof rooms," Josh explained. "Come on." He took her arm and led her toward the one empty cubicle. "Open," he said. As they approached, the glass doors swung open.

Josh urged her through them. "Lights," he said. "Dim fifty percent." The lights dimmed.

"That's…uh…impressive," Amanda said inadequately.

"Hey, that's just the easy stuff." He gestured toward the desk, where a television, a VCR and a radio sat side by side. "Television," Josh said. "Channel Four. Mute sound."

Amanda stared in astonishment as the appliance followed orders.

"It's part of the smart house concept," Josh explained. "I'm working with a builder now. Someday all this will be standard features in new houses."

Amanda turned around the room, staring in awe at what she was seeing. "It's remarkable," she said inadequately.

"They aren't just high-tech toys, Amanda, although that's how a lot of people see them," he said, brimming with excitement. "There are other people who would see them as a great deal more. People who have problems with mobility, for example. Voice-controlled units would make life a lot easier for them."

It struck Amanda how wonderful this would be for someone in that position.

"But I need a large capital investment to get this from the preliminary stages into full production. And to do that, I need you."

"I don't know, Josh. I..."

"I wouldn't expect you to do it for nothing, Amanda."

'Oh?" Amanda's annoyance returned in full force. Brandy was right. This guy was a real creep. Next to him, Dwight and Kyle were saints! "What are you suggesting? That you *pay* me to date you? Because if you are..."

Josh held up a hand. "Not money, no. That would be a little...tacky, wouldn't it?"

"Yes, it would."

"I thought so. But I do have something else." He put a hand in his pocket and pulled out a piece of paper. "I made a few phone calls this morning. Friends of mine. Business acquaintances."

Amanda eyed the list. "Why? So you could tell them we were living together, too?"

Josh grinned. "No. I'll let them hear that on the street like everyone else. I just found out which ones were planning business functions in the near future—functions that would require an executive services company." He raised an eyebrow. "You help me. I'll help you."

Amanda stared at the list. This was more than a foot in the door. This was a whole body in the door. "This is more extortion, isn't it?"

He smiled. "Actually, I think it's more like a bribe."

"It's a pretty good one," Amanda admitted.

"It is, isn't it?" He looked pleased with himself. "And it wouldn't be all that difficult for you. You simply have to do what you agreed to in the first place. Handle this Christmas present stuff. Arrange my office Christmas party. Attend a couple of business things with me. And let people go on thinking you're my...significant other for a while."

Amanda hesitated, amazed at herself for even considering it. "How long would this go on?"

"Not all that long," Josh assured her. "Just up until after my office Christmas party."

"Your office Christmas party? But that's December twenty-third."

"Perfect," said Josh. "Then you'll be free to go back to the North Pole on Christmas Eve to give Santa a hand."

Amanda studied him. He was lounging against the wall, looking cool and confident and sure of himself. He's far too accustomed to getting his own way, Edwina had told her. And Edwina was right.

Still, it was an offer that was almost impossible to refuse. Not only would she be helping their business, she'd also be helping a lot of other people who really needed help. Plus there was his family to consider. Edwina already thought Amanda and Josh were living together—and she could very well be spreading that information to the rest of his family. Apart from telling them the entire story, there wasn't much Amanda could do about that. Besides, if everyone reacted the same way as Edwina, they'd all be thrilled that Josh had a relationship. Would it be so terrible if she let them go on being thrilled a little while longer?

She didn't really have to do that much more than she'd already agreed to do. All she had to do was play the part of his girlfriend for the rest of the month, attend a couple of business functions, organize an office Christmas party, and find out something personal about every one of his relatives...all without getting too involved with Josh or his family.

"Well," she said. "I suppose..."

And then she stopped. Maybe it was the hint of triumph in Josh's eyes—or perhaps it was the fact that she'd been held hostage in her apartment all morning by his relatives. Or maybe it was simply because of her recent lunch with his mother. But it suddenly occurred to Amanda that she might just be able to use this situation to get Edwina—and the rest of Josh's family—what they all really wanted for Christmas. A little more time with him.

Don't get involved, Brandy had told her. Amanda decided to throw caution to the winds. "If I'm going to do this, I'm going to need some help."

Josh looked faintly alarmed. "What sort of help?"

"I'm going to need to know a little more about your family if I'm going to get them decent Christmas presents. It seems to me that you could help me out in that area."

Josh shoved a hand through his hair. "How? I've already told you everything I know about them."

Amanda pursed her lips. "I'm sure if you spent a little more time with them, you could find out a little more."

Josh's eyes widened. "That sounds a lot like blackmail."

"No," Amanda corrected. "Actually I believe it comes more under the heading of extortion."

Josh stared at her in outright surprise. Then he chuckled. "You catch on fast, don't you?"

"Yes, I do," said Amanda, already a little appalled at her own audacity. "Us elves are a pretty clever bunch."

"I must remember that." He grinned. "Yeah, okay. I guess I deserve it. Although you didn't have to resort to extortion to do it. I was thinking something along those lines myself."

It was Amanda's turn to be surprised. "You were?"

"Uh-huh. I do have an awful lot of relatives. It was unreasonable to expect you to find out something personal about them all by yourself, in one evening. And I'm sure I can find out a few things. I did figure out that Uncle Frank is an investment counselor."

"Yes, you did," Amanda agreed, hiding her smile.

"Besides, they are my relatives. I suppose I should know something personal about them."

"You certainly should," Amanda agreed.

Josh winced. "Okay, I'll tell you what. How about if we go to a couple more of these family things?

That would give us both a chance to find out personal things about people.''

Amanda felt a surge of triumph that almost immediately faded. "We? I didn't mean…"

"Hey, you're the elf around here. If I have to go, you have to go." He tugged on his bottom lip. "Besides, I suppose if we want people to think we're a couple, we should go a few places as a couple."

That's just what she needed…to go a few more places with him. "I suppose so," she said. "But…"

"Terrific," said Josh. "I guess we're now officially living together."

"Right," said Amanda. He started to move toward her and she took a tentative step back. "But I want to make it perfectly clear that this is strictly a business relationship."

"A business relationship," Josh repeated. He stopped where he was, his gaze met hers, he smiled his slow, sexy smile, and although there was an entire room between them, Amanda was positive she could feel the heat emanating from his body. "Of course. What else would it be?"

"What else, indeed," Amanda murmured.

6

"I DON'T LIKE THIS," Brandy said.

She was sitting in one of the chairs in Amanda's living room, radiating disapproval. "It might have been better if you'd turned down the business, given the guy a good hard smack, and left."

"I couldn't do that," Amanda insisted, although she was already half wishing that she had. "There was that list of contacts...this room filled with the most wonderful equipment that would help thousands of people...and it was the perfect opportunity to get Josh to spend more time with his family. I just couldn't say no."

"Maybe you should have tried harder," Brandy suggested. "It sounds to me as if this guy just wants to get you into a bedroom! Conning you into pretending to live with him. Really!"

"Getting me into a bedroom is the farthest thing from Josh's mind," Amanda assured her. "And it's not as if I'm really going to be living with him. He told me quite specifically that I didn't have to move in." She felt a small burst of feminine pique at that. He hadn't even tried to talk her into moving in. Not that she would have done it, but...

"That was big of him," Brandy grunted. "Look, Amanda, I do understand why you're doing this. And I certainly appreciate what it could do for our business. But you didn't have to go to these lengths to do it. As it turns out, I managed to get a little business for us myself this afternoon.''

''Oh?''

''Yes, I...uh...'' Brandy looked a little sheepish. ''I agreed to do Harvy Denton's office party for him.''

Amanda was astonished by that. ''You *what?*''

''He called again while you were out, and I decided the only way to get rid of him was to see him again.''

''You should have waited for me, Brandy. I...''

''I was pretty sure I could handle Harvy. And nothing happened.'' Brandy's lips flickered into a smile. ''He had his receptionist stay in the room with us the whole time. I stood at the door. Harvy stood at the far end of his office, with his hands held up in front of his chest. It looked as if he was afraid I'd attack him!'' She shrugged. ''He apologized...again! Then he asked me if we'd consider handling the Denton Christmas party.''

''And you said yes?'' Amanda exclaimed. ''I thought you weren't going to have anything to do with the guy.''

''I wasn't.'' Brandy looked guilty. ''But he seemed so...pathetic, Amanda. And we do need the business.''

''See,'' Amanda said. ''You're doing the same thing I'm doing.''

''Am not,'' Brandy said. ''This is strictly a business deal. I'm not getting involved with the guy.''

''I'm not getting involved, either,'' said Amanda. She thought about Josh's slow, sexy smile and drew in a breath. Brandy was right. The last thing she wanted to do was get involved with Josh Larkland, in any way, shape or form. He was too attractive—and he seemed to be able to talk her into anything. He also had heartbreaker written all over him. From the sound of things, he hadn't had a serious relationship in his life, and Amanda wasn't dumb enough to think he'd start with her. The only reason he was going through this charade was because of his business. "This is strictly a business deal, too. We're just pretending to be involved. And it's only going to be until Christmas."

"Just be careful," Brandy warned. "You don't want to find a broken heart in your stocking Christmas morning."

IT WASN'T A BROKEN HEART Amanda was worried about a couple of days later.

It was a lump of coal.

She walked along between Marilla and her husband Tom, feeling worse and worse with each step. It wasn't because of the cat show they were attending, although she had discovered that an hour of looking at cats was more than enough. It was because she felt so immensely, immensely guilty.

It was a familiar feeling. Amanda had felt that way when she'd had lunch with Edwina, and yesterday when she'd had tea with Josh's aunt Judith. Today it was stronger than ever.

If she'd had any sense, she would have said no when Marilla called this morning and invited her attend the cat show with them. "I'm sure you'll enjoy it," Marilla had assured her. "Besides, it will give us a chance to get to know each other." Amanda hadn't been able to think of a reason to refuse.

Now she wished she'd tried harder.

They stopped beside a cage holding two fluffy silver animals. "These are excellent Persians," Marilla advised. "Aren't they lovely?"

"Spectacular," Amanda said. She glanced around the crowded auditorium. "I had no idea there were this many different kinds of cats in the world."

"There are hundreds of species," Marilla announced. She took Amanda's arm. "I'm so pleased that Josh met someone like you, Amanda."

"Are you?" Amanda said. She wasn't. As a matter of fact, she was beginning to regret she'd ever laid eyes on the man.

"Yes. That's what we all want for Josh. For him to settle down—and raise a family."

"A family?" Amanda repeated. She closed her eyes and issued a fervent prayer that Marilla wouldn't suggest this to Josh. He might tell her that kids were on their way, just to make his relatives all happy. Then he'd expect Amanda to produce a few—all before Christmas! "We aren't even close to the family stage," she said.

"I'm sure it will come up." Marilla squeezed Amanda's arm. "You know, Amanda, there are times when Tom and I find Josh a little intimidating. Don't we, Tom?"

"We certainly do," Tom said.

Since Tom had spent the entire afternoon agreeing with Marilla, Amanda wasn't too surprised at his response. However, she was surprised by Marilla's comment. Amanda didn't consider Josh intimidating. Insensitive, yes. Intimidating, no.

"Intimidating?" she asked.

"Sometimes. He's so...clever. Not that we're not

clever, but...well, he's clever in a different direction. Isn't he, Tom?''

"Sure is," Tom said.

"He's always been like that," Marilla confided. "Not that I know him that well. There's quite a few years between us, so we didn't really grow up together. When Dad married Edwina, I was already away from home, taking my veterinary assistant course.''

"Oh." Amanda blinked. So that's what she did.

"I did used to take care of him sometimes, though. He used to come and stay with me when Dad and Edwina went off for a holiday." She chuckled. "He was very fond of that Sphinx cat I had. His name was Fitzgerald, but for some reason Josh called him Fluffy." Her face curled into confusion. "I never did understand it, because that particular breed is completely hairless.''

"Really?" Amanda said, trying to repress a smile.

"We lost poor Fitzgerald last year. He contracted a serious case of pneumonia and we just couldn't save him.''

"Oh," Amanda said faintly. "I'm...um...terribly sorry.''

"It was a tragedy," Marilla agreed. "But now we have Algonquin. I'm not sure Josh has ever met him. We don't see much of him these days." She patted Amanda's arm. "Of course, now that you're part of his life, I'm sure we'll see him a lot more." They paused beside another cage. "Look at this Burmese. Doesn't it just take your breath away?''

"Definitely," Amanda said.

She'd never felt like such a low-life in her whole life.

JOSH WALKED into the lobby of his office the next afternoon to find Mable standing beside a fully decorated Christmas tree that seemed to have materialized in the corner opposite her desk.

"Has that always been here?" Josh asked as he stopped to admire it.

"No," said Mable. She adjusted an ornament. "We've never had one in here before. I have suggested putting one up a few times but you usually say something touching and Christmassy like 'Over my dead body.'"

"Oh," Josh said. "Well, I didn't know it would look this attractive." He glanced over at Mable. "Did you put it up?"

"I helped," Mable said modestly. "But Amanda did most of it."

"Amanda?" Of course, Amanda. He'd thought he'd caught a whiff of her perfume when he'd stepped off the elevator. He smiled. He should have known his Christmas elf would be behind a Christmas tree. He glanced down the hall. "Where is she?"

"She just left." Mable returned to her desk. "I must say, I'm glad I called that executive services company. Amanda is exactly what we need around here." She frowned up at Josh. "That doesn't mean I like what you're doing with her."

Josh grimaced. He'd told Mable about his arrangement with Amanda, on the off chance that his business acquaintances would ask her about it. Mable didn't approve, and she'd been very vocal about it. "I'm not doing anything with her. As a matter of fact, I've hardly seen her." That was certainly true. He hadn't seen much of Amanda at all these past couple of days. He knew she'd been working with Mable on making arrangements for the office Christmas party, but she seemed to come and go when he wasn't around, or had been too busy to notice. He had spoken with her a few times on the phone, to pass on social arrangements, or to check on her Christmas present progress. That wasn't strictly necessary, since his family kept him up to date on her activities. "I just had tea with Amanda," Aunt Judith had enthused. "I do like her, Josh. And I love the towels she has in her bathroom."

"Amanda came to the cat show with me," Marilla had informed him this morning. "She's thinking of getting a Siamese."

It seems the only person who didn't see Amanda was him. "You don't think she's…avoiding me, do you?" he asked Mable.

"I have no idea," said Mable. "But I wouldn't blame her if she was. *I'd* avoid you if I were her."

"You would?" Josh didn't understand that. "Why?"

Mable gave him an impatient look. "Well, you haven't treated her very nicely, have you? First you con her into doing your Christmas shopping for you. Then you con her into pretending she's you're girlfriend. She's probably wondering what else you're going to try to con her into."

Josh stroked a hand around his chin. "What does that mean?"

"You're telling people that you two are living together. She might think that you're planning on…taking advantage of the situation."

"Taking advantage of the situation?" Josh blinked a few times. "Me?"

Mable smiled slightly. "She doesn't know you very well."

"That's for sure," Josh grumbled. And if she kept avoiding him, she'd never get to know him very well.

He wandered into his office and dropped into a chair. Come to think of it, Amanda had said something about this being a business relationship. At the time he hadn't been sure what she meant. Perhaps she had been warning him not to take advantage of the situation. Of course, he'd never do anything like that. A brief memory of that kiss they'd shared flashed through his mind. He wouldn't mind repeating that experience though.

Mable had made another good point. He had used a pretty underhanded technique to get Amanda to act as his girlfriend. He couldn't really blame her if she was annoyed with him about that. However, he could make up for that by giving her a hand with this personal stuff.

He picked up the phone. Hadn't Shelby mentioned something about a party tonight? They could go to that. He could get started on this personal business right away.

AMANDA WAS STILL FEELING depressed that afternoon when Brandy rushed into her apartment. "You will never believe what just happened," Brandy exclaimed as she threw off her coat.

Amanda eyed her with some alarm. "Oh, no. Don't tell me another guy tried to jump you?"

"No," said Brandy. "No one tried to jump me. I've just met with Harvey McCormick's secretary's assistant."

"Harvey McCormick's secretary's assistant,"

Amanda repeated. She smiled vacantly at Brandy, and returned to studying her gift list. "How...nice."

"It's not just nice, Amanda. It's fabulous!"

"Is it?" Amanda considered the names in front of her. "Do you think a tie is a personal gift for a man?"

"It depends on the man. Don't you know who Harvey McCormick is?"

"No," said Amanda. "How about if the man is an uncle?"

"Then a tie is fine," said Brandy. "Amanda, Harvey McCormick is the president of the NorthRim Oil and Gas Company."

"Is he?" Amanda wrote "tie" beside Frank's name. "That explains why his secretary has an assistant. I think Josh's uncle Frank needs a new tie. The one he was wearing the other night was really old-fashioned. And it was so...blue." She tapped her pencil thoughtfully against the paper. "On the other hand, maybe all investment counselors wear old-fashioned blue ties. Do you know any?"

"Not on purpose." Brandy reached over and pulled the pencil out of Amanda's hand. "Will you pay attention here? I just met with the assistant to the secretary of the president of the NorthRim Oil and Gas Company. She wants to arrange a little function they are having for some of their corporate pals."

"Ah," said Amanda, her mind still filled with gift ideas. "That's...great."

"Great?" Brandy gave her a look of total disgust. "It's...incredible. Amanda, Harvey McCormick's idea of a 'little function' is two hundred people."

Amanda eyed her warily. "Do we have to get them Christmas presents?"

"No, we don't! We just have to organize it." She

grinned practically from ear to ear. "And they're not just any people. They're important people!"

"Are they?" said Amanda. "Well, that's...great."

Brandy peered into her face. "It could just be my imagination, but you don't seem to be sharing my enthusiasm here."

"I'm enthusiastic," Amanda assured her. "I'm happy we're getting the business, but—well, there's just so much to do. I've lined up the caterers for Josh's office party. I'm working on getting the entertainment. I've got the decorations ordered—along with a few Christmas trees and ornaments. I've phoned all over the city for that Halsone for Aunt Mimi and I've thought up a billion reasons why Josh can't go anywhere." She grimaced at the stack of invitations sitting on the sofa beside her. "I think that's the hardest part. I mean, how many ways are there to say, 'He never leaves his office'?"

"I thought he was supposed to leave his office," Brandy complained. "Isn't that the whole point of this?"

"He can't possibly go to everything." Even if he could, Amanda strongly doubted that he would. "Besides, he is coming to Shelby's with me tonight." She'd been a little surprised when Josh had called and suggested they go, although she suspected he was just trying to finish off his obligation to "give her a hand with the personal stuff." "And before you say anything, I am not, repeat not, getting involved. It's simply a business function."

"Sure," Brandy said.

"It is," Amanda insisted. She gave Brandy a hopeful look. "Why don't you come with us? I'm sure

Shelby wouldn't mind. And I could use the moral support.''

"I can't," said Brandy. "I'm busy this evening." She looked down at her hands. "I'm...um...meeting Harvy for a drink."

"Harvy?" Amanda studied Brandy's rather sheepish demeanor. "You mean...Harvy Denton?"

"Uh-huh."

"I thought you weren't going to have anything to do with him."

"I'm not," Brandy assured her. "But I've talked to him a couple of times at his office...and so far he's behaved himself. So when he suggested we get together to have a drink, I said yes, just to see what he'd do." She raised an eyebrow. "However, I plan on making it clear that I have no intention of crawling into bed with him." She sighed. "That will probably convince him to leave me alone."

"Sounds like a fun evening," said Amanda. "At least a lot more fun than trying to force Josh Larkland to find out anything personal about his relatives."

"What?"

"Let's be realistic here, Brandy. I might get Josh to one or two family get-togethers at the very most. And the possibility of him coming up with something personal about his relatives is slim to none. If he manages to discover their ages and occupations, I'll be surprised."

"So will I, but I didn't think you felt that way."

"I didn't," said Amanda. "I thought all I had to do was get Josh together with his family a little more. Now I'm starting to wonder if I even should be doing it."

"Oh?" Brandy blinked a few times. "What brought this on?"

"I was at a cat show with Marilla last night."

"Ah, a cat show." Brandy snapped her fingers. "Maybe I should have sent you to one of those before you went into Josh's office."

Amanda ignored her. "Marilla told me that she used to baby-sit Josh when he was younger. Now she hardly ever sees him." She gave Brandy an anguished look. "So far, every single one of his relatives has told me the same thing. They're all crazy about him, but they just don't see him anymore. And they're all so eager to meet me and they just hope that now he has a relationship he'll spend more time with them."

"So?"

"So he doesn't have a relationship! He's hired me, and I blackmailed him into spending a little time with his family. If this doesn't work, they are all going to be really disappointed, and I'm going to feel terrible." She sighed. "I don't know what possessed me to take a job as a Christmas elf in the first place."

AT FIVE O'CLOCK, Mable walked into Josh's office and came to a full stop in the doorway. "What happened in here?" she asked.

Josh took a look around. His computers were switched off, the test equipment was put away, and his papers were neatly stacked on his desk. "Nothing," he said. "I'm just leaving."

"You're leaving?" Mable checked her watch. "But it's just five o'clock."

"I know," said Josh. "I have to leave now. We're going to Shelby's tonight, and she lives miles away from the city. I have to go home, change, and pick up Amanda—and a map.''

"Shelby?'' Mable repeated. "You mean, your sister Shelby? The one who teaches at the university?''

"Uh-huh,'' he said, looking quizzically at Mable. So that's what Shelby did. He'd known it had something to do with children.

Mable's forehead furrowed. "You know, Josh, this is the second family thing you've gone to in a week. Is there something wrong that you haven't told me about, or are you just trying to set a world record?''

"No,'' said Josh. "I'm giving Amanda a hand—at finding out personal things about people.''

"Oh.'' Mable's lips twitched slightly. "That's... uh...decent of you.''

Josh put on his coat. "They are my relatives, Mable, and there are a lot of them. I can't expect Amanda to do it all by herself.''

"Right,'' said Mable. "Well, it's...uh...nice of you to sacrifice yourself.'' She walked out of the office, shaking her head.

IT'S A BUSINESS FUNCTION, Amanda told herself.

However, when she opened her door and saw Josh standing on the other side, it was very difficult to remember that.

He stood in the entranceway and studied her from head to toe. "You look nice,'' he said. "Very elf-like.''

Amanda flushed with pleasure at the compliment. "You look nice, too.'' He looked more than nice. He looked scrumptious, dressed in a long brown parka, which he hadn't buttoned up, a pair of dress pants, and a white-and-gray shirt under a dark blue sweater. "That's a great sweater."

"Is it?" He shrugged. "I think my mother gave it to me. Or one of my sisters. Or maybe an aunt." He glanced around her small place with outright curiosity. "You know what," he said. "This does look like an elf lives here, except the doors are normal size."

Amanda glanced over her shoulder, taking in the small, square living room with the odd bits of furniture her grandmother had given her—a small, dark-oak coffee table with matching end tables, a white-and-green-striped couch, the minuscule Christmas tree in the corner—their papers spread over the coffee table. "A messy elf," Amanda confessed. "We're using my entire apartment as an office until we can afford a real one."

Brandy came out of the kitchen while she was pulling on her coat. Amanda introduced them. "This is my partner, Brandy Bradford. Brandy, this is Josh Larkland."

"Hi," Josh said. He smiled his charming smile and shook Brandy's hand. "Mandy and Brandy. The Christmas elves. You even look like one, too."

Brandy scowled at him. "It's not polite to make remarks about people's height. And for your information, I am not short. I am vertically challenged." She turned to Amanda. "Remember, you can't reform them." She nodded at Josh, and stomped into the living room.

Josh stared after her. "Was it something I said?"

"Don't mind Brandy," Amanda advised as she took her coat out of the closet. "She's just having a...a bad elf day."

"Oh," Josh said. He helped Amanda on with her

coat, his breath warm against her neck. "I hope it isn't contagious. Otherwise it could be a very long evening."

IF THE DRIVE to Shelby's place was any indication, it was going to be an extremely long evening.

"Are you positive you know where she lives?" Amanda asked as she peered out the window. The city was receding rapidly out the back window, there didn't seem to be very many lights out here, and Amanda was starting to wish she'd found another means of transportation.

That wasn't just because of the drive. Being alone with Josh in the dark intimacy of the car just reminded her of how attractive he was. She had to keep looking out the window to stop herself from admiring his profile, the way his hands curled around the steering wheel, or the movement of his thigh when he pressed on the brakes.

"Of course I know where she lives," said Josh. "I have been here before, you know."

"Really?" Amanda studied him. "When was that?"

"I'm...not sure. In the fall, I think. Or maybe it was spring."

"More likely two years ago," Amanda muttered.

Josh glanced over at her and frowned. "Don't worry. I'm not going to get you lost." He stretched out an arm to ruffle her hair. "God knows what Santa would do to me if I lost one of his elves."

If he didn't stop touching her, Amanda wasn't sure what she'd do to him. Just the feel of his hand on her hair made her dizzy.

"Is Brandy your roommate?" he asked after a moment.

"Not anymore," said Amanda. "She's been a friend for a long time. When she broke up with her boyfriend she moved in with me for a few months, but now she has a place of her own."

"Oh," Josh said. "Well, it was nice of you to help her out."

"She's my friend," said Amanda. "Naturally I wanted to help her out. That's what friends are for." She paused, then added pointedly, "That's what families are for, too."

"Of course they are," Josh said easily. "And speaking of family, I hear you were at a cat show yesterday with Marilla."

"Oh? How did you hear that?"

"The family grapevine keeps me informed." He glanced over at her. "How did that go? Did you find out anything personal about her?"

"Only that she really, really likes cats, she used to have one named Fitzgerald, and that she finds you intimidating."

"Intimidating? Me?" He chuckled. "I wouldn't call myself intimidating." He glanced over at her. "What do you mean she *used* to have a cat named Fitzgerald?"

"He got pneumonia."

"Fluffy got pneumonia?" Josh's eyes widened. "Poor Marilla. She must be really upset."

"I think she's getting over it," said Amanda. "After all, it did happen last year."

"Oh," said Josh. "I didn't know that." His forehead furrowed. "I don't know why people don't tell me these things." He stopped the car in front of an enormous house that seemed to have appeared from out of nowhere. "Oh, no," he said.

Amanda took a quick look around, but couldn't spot anything unusual. "What's the matter?" she asked. "Isn't this the place?"

"No, this is the place, all right." Josh looked over at her and grimaced. "I've just remembered a couple of personal things about Shelby."

"What?" asked Amanda.

"Well, for one thing she's a university professor." He switched off the engine and opened his door. "And for another…she's a lousy cook."

UNFORTUNATELY, Josh was right.

Amanda stood in Shelby's kitchen and eyed the tray Shelby was pulling out of the oven. "They're crab canapés," Shelby explained. "It's a variation of a recipe I got when I was in Tucson a few years ago. I discovered that the addition of a little Tabasco sauce and a few jalapeno peppers really spices it up."

"They look…uh…interesting," Amanda said, then began to arrange the canapés on a platter. "I really like your house, Shelby. It's beautiful. And it's the perfect place to raise a family."

"We like it," said Shelby. "Although the drive out here can get exhausting. I seem to spend half my life on that highway." She paused. "You know, I'd almost forgotten that you hadn't been out here before. You seem to belong with us, if you know what I mean."

Amanda shifted uncomfortably. "Well…uh… thank you, but…um…I'm not exactly—"

"And I'm so pleased about it, too," Shelby went

on. "It's so nice to see Josh out and about again. He seems to spend his entire life in his office—at least that's where I assume he is," she said dryly. "My children have even suggested that their uncle Josh might be an agent."

"An agent?"

"A secret agent," Shelby explained.

"You mean, a spy?" Amanda bit down on her lip. In that profession he probably wouldn't last more than a day. On the other hand, when she'd left Josh in the living room a little while ago, he'd been pumping Shelby's husband Gordon for information. "So, Gordon," he'd been saying. "Tell me. What exactly is it that you do?"

Come to think of it, he was sort of acting like a cloak-and-dagger Christmas agent.

"Yes." Shelby shoved another cooking platter into the oven. "On our side, of course."

"Of course," said Amanda.

"I know it seems far-fetched. But he has all the signs. He's never around, no one understands what he does, and we don't see much of him." She waved around an oven-mitted hand. "He does behave like he's a spy, doesn't he?"

Amanda focused on the platter she was creating. "I suppose he does."

"For a while I almost believed it myself," Shelby continued. "I think I wanted to. It's much better than the truth."

"The truth?"

"You know. That he just isn't very interested in us."

Amanda looked over her shoulder at Shelby's earnest face. "I'm sure he's interested in you, Shelby."

"Not really," said Shelby. "Months go by when no one hears from him, and we seldom see him anymore. I think the party at Mimi's was the first time I've seen him since the summer. And I can't remember the last time he was out here. Today he even had to ask me for directions."

Amanda narrowed her eyes. "Oh, he did, did he?"

"Of course, I can't remember the last time I was at his place, either. And I have no idea what he does. I have asked but he says something like 'network throughput factors.' I don't know what any of those words mean."

"Neither do I," Amanda admitted.

"Of course, Josh has always been like that," Shelby continued. "Even when he was young I couldn't follow what he was doing."

Amanda found the idea of a little Josh incredibly interesting. "Really?"

"Oh, yes. He was always wiring things up in the most amazing ways. At one point he had half the house wired up to the television remote control. The only way you could make toast was to turn the television to channel three." She busied herself doing something with salmon. "Of course, that might have been because of his father."

Amanda hadn't followed that. "His father?"

"Yes. He was in some sort of car accident, you know."

"No," Amanda said. "No, I didn't know that."

"Well, he was. Of course, I never met him. He passed away before Dad met Edwina. But I understand that he was pretty crippled by it. He found it difficult to get around."

Amanda was just digesting that when Josh wandered into the room. "Gordon's been showing me your computer," he confessed. "I reconfigured your memory, fixed the lost clusters on your hard drive, and got your printer working."

Shelby stared at him. "You did? That hasn't been working for six months."

"That's what Gordon said." Josh shook his head. "You should have fixed it a long time ago, Shel. It wasn't that hard to do."

"I certainly don't know how. And neither does Gordon."

"Yeah, but I do." Josh washed the black toner off his hands at the sink. "I don't know why you people don't call me when you have problems like this."

"I...uh...just didn't want to bother you," Shelby stammered. "You're busy and..."

"You're my sister, Shelby," Josh said patiently. "I'm never too busy to help you out. After all, that is what families are for." His gaze met Amanda's over Shelby's head, and he gave her a smug smile before glancing down at the canapé tray in her hand. His eyes widened, and he cleared his throat. "Well...uh...this has been great, Shelby, but I'm afraid we're going to have to leave now."

"But it's only ten o'clock," Shelby objected. "And you've hardly eaten anything. I..."

"I know," said Josh. "But we have to get home. Amanda has a headache."

"She does?" Shelby glanced at Amanda. "She didn't mention it to me."

"She didn't mention it to me, either," said Josh. He put an arm around Amanda. "But all I have to do is look at her and I know she isn't feeling well."

"ALL YOU HAVE TO DO is look at me and you know I'm not feeling well?" Amanda repeated incredulously. She took a bite out of her hamburger and frowned at Josh. "I can't believe you actually said that."

Josh's eyes gleamed with amusement. "Hey, if we're going to go places as a couple there are some things we should know about each other. Besides, I was getting hungry...and I wasn't going to eat that. Was it my imagination, or was there fish in everything she served?"

"There was a lot of fish," Amanda admitted. "Shelby said it was brain food."

"My brain wasn't getting full on it." Josh set down his hamburger while he took a sip of his Coke. He'd stopped at the first fast-food place they'd come to, insisting that he was going to perish if he didn't have something to eat. "Let's give her a cookbook for Christmas."

"We can't do that!"

"Why not?" Josh asked. "Isn't it personal?"

Amanda hesitated. "Actually, it's a little too personal."

"Oh," he said. "Well, how about if we give it to Gordon, then?"

"No. In Gordon's case it wouldn't be personal enough."

"This is really complicated," Josh complained. "Ornaments are personal, cookbooks are too personal, or not personal enough. Who writes the rules on this stuff?"

"No one writes them," said Amanda. "Everybody just knows them."

"I don't," said Josh. He smiled into her eyes. "It's a good thing I've got you around."

Amanda averted her gaze. *Don't you dare come on to me, Josh Larkland,* she thought. *I just might go along with it.* She knew how that would end. She'd get too intense and he wouldn't even know it had happened.

"Shelby could sure use some new computer equipment," Josh said after a moment. "I don't know why she didn't call me to take a look at it before."

"Perhaps she didn't think you'd be interested in her problems," Amanda suggested.

Josh looked shocked. "Of course I'm interested! She's my sister. I'm interested in her."

"Maybe she doesn't know that. After all, it doesn't sound as if you spend much time with her."

Josh lowered his eyelids. "I spend time with her. Besides, I'm…busy." He was silent for a moment. "You know what I'd like to give Shelby? A ten-gig hard drive, some extra RAM memory and a fast data/fax modem. Would that be personal?"

"It depends what it is," said Amanda. "I didn't understand a word you said."

"It's what Shelby needs to bring that computer of theirs up to date." He leaned back in his chair. "Gordon told me that Shelby spends a lot of time driving back to the university at night to use the Internet. With some new equipment, she'd get better response time at home, and she wouldn't have to do that. I'd even volunteer to come out and install it—as long as it's after lunch and before dinner."

"You would?"

"Of course, I would. She's my sister, Amanda. I'd like to help her out."

"Oh," said Amanda. "Well, in that case, I'd say it's very personal. And very thoughtful."

"It is?" Josh looked both pleased and surprised. "Hey, maybe I'm getting the hang of this, after all."

Amanda watched him munch away on his hamburger. Maybe he was getting the hang of this.

When Josh stopped his car in front of her apartment building, switched off the engine, and started to get out, Amanda put a hand on his arm to hold him back. "Thank you for taking me," she said. "But there's no need for you to get out."

He turned his head toward her, with a quizzical expression on his face.

"This is a business arrangement, Josh," Amanda reminded him. "I think we should keep it that way."

JOSH WAS DEEP in thought when Mable walked into his office the next morning.

"So?" she asked. "How was the party last night?"

"Not too bad," Josh said.

"Did you...uh...find out anything personal about anyone?"

"Yup," Josh said. "Shelby serves a lot of fish, she doesn't know anything about computers, and Fluffy got pneumonia."

"Oh," said Mable. "Well, I suppose that's something."

She was on her way out the door when Josh called her back. "Tell me something, Mabe. Would you call me intimidating?"

"Intimidating?" Mable turned to face him and released a bark of laughter. "No, I certainly wouldn't. Obnoxious, maybe. Overbearing. Sometimes belligerent. Intelligent, of course, but..."

Josh scowled at her. "I wasn't asking for a personal critique. I was asking about intimidating."

"Oh," said Mable. "Well, in that case, no. I don't think you're particularly intimidating." She gave him a curious look. "Why?"

"Marilla told Amanda she thinks I'm intimidating."

"Oh," said Mable. "Well, I'd say Marilla doesn't know you very well."

"That's what I thought," Josh muttered. He watched Mable walk out of his office, then pushed himself out of his chair and wandered over to the window. He had found out a few more personal things last night, but they were mostly about himself.

For one thing, he hadn't expected Amanda to practically leap out of his car when he took her home, after coolly advising him that she thought they should keep their relationship strictly business. He hadn't realized how much he'd been anticipating another of those tantalizing kisses of hers.

However, now that he thought about it Amanda was probably right. They should keep their relationship strictly business. If they didn't, it could turn into a relationship sort of relationship, and Josh wanted no part of that. He'd been in enough of those to know how they turned out. As soon as he started dating a woman, she expected him to do things like go out every night, or show up someplace on time...and she'd get annoyed when he didn't do it. He didn't want that to happen with Amanda. She was his Christmas elf, and that's all he wanted her to be.

He shoved aside the niggling suspicion that he wasn't being completely honest about that and concentrated on his family.

For some time they had been telling him that they didn't see enough of him. He had thought they were exaggerating, but he was starting to wonder if maybe they were right. There sure seemed to be a lot of things he didn't know about them. He couldn't remember the last time he was at Shelby's. He hadn't even known she owned a computer, much less needed help with it. She hadn't called him to give her a hand, either. Marilla thought he was intimidating and she hadn't told him that cat of hers had gotten pneumonia.

Maybe he was a little out of touch with his relatives. There was a good reason for that, though, he thought furiously. He had a lot to do! It certainly wasn't that he wasn't interested in them or didn't care about them. He was just...busy.

Still, he wasn't busy tonight, was he?

He checked his calendar, then picked up the phone. Maybe he should go to another one of these family things. After all, he was getting the hang of this personal stuff. And he was curious to see what his family hadn't gotten around to telling him.

"HOW DID THINGS with Harvy go last night?" Amanda asked Brandy. They were stretched at either ends of the couch in Amanda's living room. "He didn't try to jump you, did he?"

"No, he didn't." Brandy said, sounding puzzled. "He actually behaved like a gentleman. I told him flat-out that I wasn't sleeping with him and he seemed...relieved." Brandy massaged the back of her neck like she had a major kink in it.

"Relieved?"

"Uh-huh," Brandy said. "Then we had a couple

of drinks...we talked...and he took me home. He didn't even try to *kiss* me!"

"See," Amanda said. "Maybe you were wrong about him."

"Maybe." Brandy didn't sound convinced. "Or maybe he was trying out a new technique on me." Still rubbing her neck, she gave Amanda a penetrating look. "How was your *date?*"

"It wasn't a date," Amanda said too quickly. "It was a business function. And it went a lot better than I expected. Josh did find out something personal about Shelby."

"Her age and occupation?" Brandy teased.

"No. He already knew that." Amanda told her all about the computer equipment. "It sounds like a great present. And it's exactly what Shelby needs."

"I suppose that's something," Brandy admitted grudgingly.

"It's more than something," Amanda insisted. "This just might work, Brandy. He found out something personal about one person." She leaned back. "He seemed interested in Shelby, too. He seemed as if he cared about her. Not only that, but this morning he called and said he wanted to go to a few more family things—so he can find out more personal stuff about people." She smiled. "However, he also added that he wants me to find out what they're serving before I say we'll come."

"*We'll* come?" Brandy stressed, raising an eyebrow. "You mean, you're going to go out with him *again?*"

"I have to," said Amanda. "After all, we are supposed to be a couple." She caught Brandy's frown and sighed. "It's strictly a business arrangement, Brandy."

"Does Josh know that?"

"Yes, he does," Amanda said, trying to sound cool and casual. "I made it very clear to him last night." She felt a pang of regret at that. She would have enjoyed another one of his kisses.

"What about you?" Brandy asked. "Do you still remember it's strictly a business arrangement?"

"Of course. That's exactly what it is," she said, her voice quivering slightly. She snuck a glance in Brandy's direction. Brandy appeared unconvinced. Her relationship with Josh was strictly business, right? So why did her voice quiver every time she said his name, and why did the memory of his kiss keep replaying over and over again?

7

"LET'S SEE," Amanda said.

She sat in Josh's office, a calendar on her lap, along with her lists. "We've got Frank and Louise's party, Aunt Francine's open house, and your cousin Glenda's barbecue…" She paused. "Does your cousin really have a barbecue in December?"

Josh shrugged. "I guess we'll find out. Go on."

"Okay." Amanda referred back to her book. "Then your mother is having a few people over, and we've been invited to drop by Hemp's place for drinks. Oh, and we've also got Hank Turnbull's open house. You said you wanted to go to that."

"I do." Josh gave her a hopeful look. "I don't suppose you know what they're going to be…"

"No, I don't," Amanda interrupted. "I have not yet found a polite way of saying 'I'll come to your Christmas thing if you tell me what you're serving and it better not be fish.'"

"Too bad." Josh lounged back in his office chair. "I don't suppose you could just *ask?*"

"Absolutely not," Amanda said firmly. "It would be considered rude."

"What? Aren't there any rude elves in the world?"

"Not a single one," said Amanda. "We are all a very polite bunch."

"Darn," said Josh, and he looked so cute and disgruntled that Amanda completely lost track of the conversation and had to refer back to her notes.

It was a familiar problem. She had it frequently when she was with Josh, and she had only herself to blame. She'd wanted him to get involved with his family. Well, he was definitely doing that—and he was taking her along with him.

Josh had been pretty accurate when he'd said that he was a fast worker when he made up his mind. Apparently he'd made up his mind to find out personal things about his relatives. And he was now charging at it, full steam ahead.

Since Shelby's party, they'd been to a family dinner at his aunt Sofia's, where he'd discovered that Sofia liked Frank Sinatra records, an open house at Judith's, where they'd spent most of the evening looking at old family photographs and talking about bathrooms, and had even stopped by Marilla's for drinks. Josh had taken Marilla flowers. "I was really sorry to hear about Fluffy," he'd said as he'd handed them over. Then he'd spent the rest of the evening trying not to act intimidating.

Amanda was doing everything she could to keep her dealings with Josh as businesslike as possible, but it was difficult. Josh was difficult. He phoned her three or four times a day to check their schedule, to throw in some brainstorm he'd had that might possibly be personal, or sometimes, it seemed, just to talk.

He'd insisted that she accompany him to every social event. "We're supposed to be a couple," he'd reminded her. "That means we go to these things together." Sometimes Amanda thought that might be because he wanted to be with her, although the more realistic part of her knew it was because he wanted them to be seen as a couple, and because he considered it part of her job to go. He also used her as an excuse to leave when he'd had enough. "We have to go now," he'd say. "Amanda has to be at work early." Then he'd add, in an undertone, "Elves need lots of sleep."

"We don't have to go to every single function, you know," she told him. "We could miss a few."

"Christmas isn't that far away...and we've still got a lot of people to go—including my mother." He drew his eyebrows together. "I don't suppose you've come up with any good ideas for her yet."

"I've come up with a lot of good ideas for her," Amanda objected. "*You* just don't like any of them."

"I just don't *understand* them. How can a watch be personal? Everyone in the world has one. It has to be as bad as giving everybody the same perfume."

"It isn't, but..."

"And a pasta maker?" He frowned at her. "I didn't even know what a pasta maker was until you told me. And even then, I don't see what's personal about it. Spaghetti just doesn't do it for me. If I built a voice-activated one, it might be, but..."

"Forget the pasta maker," Amanda said quickly. "I'm sure we can come up with something else." She paused. "There's no reason for us both to go to these things. You are getting really good at this. I'm sure if you went..."

"No." Josh folded his arms and looked stubborn. "You're the Christmas elf around here. If I have to go, you have to go." He paused, then added, "Besides, those things are more fun when you are there. I almost enjoy them."

He looked puzzled by that, as if he wasn't expecting it. Amanda's body tingled at the words, a tingle that faded when he added, "And it gives me a good excuse to leave when I want."

"Just make sure you tell me which excuse you use," Amanda warned. "The other night you told everyone we had to leave because I wasn't feeling well. The next morning, when everyone called to see how I was, I had no idea what they were talking about." She'd been particularly flummoxed when Aunt Judith had called her to see if the rabbit had died. It had taken Amanda a good minute to realize Judith was hinting that she might be pregnant—a suggestion Amanda had vehemently denied. The last thing she needed was for Mimi to make that suggestion to Josh. She wouldn't be one bit surprised if Josh said she was, just to make his family happy! Then nine months from now, he'd probably demand that she produce an offspring.

She smiled at the image, then almost immediately sobered up. Nine months from now she wouldn't be seeing Josh or his family. As a matter of fact, in just under two weeks she wouldn't be seeing them. By Christmas Eve, their work was through.

The prospect made her suddenly feel cold. She flipped over a page in her notebook, and turned her attention back to business. "All right. We both go. Now let's discuss your Christmas party. I've arranged for a string quartet and a piano player..."

"A piano player!" Josh said in a mock horrified tone. "Oh, no. Don't tell me we're going to have...singing?"

"THERE'S THE INTERNET trade show, the Vistech open house, and the corporate gifts for the Dawson building supply company," Brandy reported later that afternoon to Amanda as they quickly gobbled down a late lunch of take-out pizza. "I have only one question. How do we clone ourselves?" Brandy said, grinning with satisfaction.

"That's a good question," Amanda agreed. There were boxes of corporate gifts and stacks of papers strewn all around her apartment. "Or I guess a better question is, how do we clone this apartment?" She rested back against the chair. "This is ridiculous. A few weeks ago we couldn't get any business. Now we almost have too much."

"That's thanks to you, Amanda," Brandy said, wiping the grease off her fingers with a napkin before she picked up her To-Do list. "Every person we contacted on that list Josh gave you has hired us to do something." She paused. "You know, Amanda, I'm starting to think I was wrong about this character. He's brought us all this business. He's paying his bills on time. And he does seem to be getting involved with his family."

"That's true," Amanda agreed. "He's going to everything there is to go to. And has come up with some wonderful presents for people. The computer equipment he got for Shelby is exactly what she needs. Of course, he's insisted on giving her some kind of computer cookbook program, too." He'd also come up with fishing equipment for his uncle Reg after he'd remembered that Reg had taken him fishing a couple of times when he was a boy.

"He's suggested some pretty bizarre things, too. He wanted to give his aunt Sofia a can of spray paint because he didn't like the colors in her house."

Amanda shuddered. "I didn't like the color, either. You should have seen it. Everything in it was cherry-red, including the toilet paper...although I think that's a gift from Aunt Judith." She paused, looking at all the work spread out in front of her. "I suppose the only down side of all this is that you're getting stuck with most of the work. I'm just...too busy."

"You sure are," Brandy agreed. "You're out with this guy almost every night."

"They're just business functions," Amanda reminded her.

"They're Larkland family functions," Brandy corrected. She furrowed her forehead. "And I must say they sure hold a lot of them. How can all the same people go to that many parties?"

"They aren't the same people," Amanda explained. "Shelby told me all about it. Everyone invites their friends over and includes their family. But no one goes to everything—although Josh is certainly giving it a good try." Amanda thought about his eyes and the feeling of his hand on her shoulder, and decided to change the subject. "How are things going with you and Harvy Denton? You seem to have been spending a lot of time with him."

"Well, yes," Brandy said with a smile. "He's really quite interesting when you get to know him." She screwed up her face. "Although I must say, I'm starting to really wonder about him."

"Why?"

"Well...it's just that all we seem to do is go out for dinner."

Amanda didn't see the significance of that. She'd been out for dinner with Josh—at his suggestion. "We both have to eat. And I'm not going to go to another one of those things on an empty stomach.'' They'd also gotten into the habit of stopping for coffee after they left a family party. At first that was just so they could compare notes about gift ideas—and also because Josh seldom liked what he'd been served. However the conversation usually digressed to discuss other things. Josh told her all about his work, and his plans for the future. Sometimes Amanda didn't understand what he was talking about, but she liked watching the sparkle in his eye when he explained it. He might be clued out about life, but when it came to his job, he was definitely clued in.

''That sounds pleasant,'' she said to Brandy.

''It is pleasant,'' Brandy said. ''But don't you think it's a little...peculiar?''

''Eating dinner isn't peculiar.''

''It is if it's all you do.''

''What do you mean?'' Amanda asked, still not getting it.

''I mean that Harvy hasn't made a pass at me. All we do is...talk.''

She looked so perplexed, Amanda had to smile. ''I thought you didn't want him to make a pass at you.''

''I didn't,'' Brandy assured her. ''But I'm starting to think that I wouldn't mind getting involved with him.'' A dreamy look crept across her face. ''He doesn't seem to be the creep I thought he was at all. He's polite and kind...and he treats me better than any man I've ever met. I'm just not sure he's interested.''

''I'm sure he is.''

''I'm not. It's a little weird. Last week he was jumping me in his office. Since then, he's taken me out three times, and he hasn't done anything more than take my arm when we're crossing the street." She paused. "Actually, I take his arm when we cross the street. I thought he was just going out with me to soften me up for another encounter, but so far he hasn't made any moves in that direction." She sighed. "What about you? Has Josh put any moves on you?"

"I don't think Josh *has* moves," Amanda said. She thought about that long-ago kiss and changed her mind. "Okay, he might have a few. But I'm sure he wouldn't use them on me." He certainly hadn't made any move to do so. He treated her with the same casual affection he used toward Mable. Oh, he did seem to drop an arm around her shoulders, or take her hand, but he only did that when they were with other people. "He treats me the same way he treats his secretary," she told Brandy.

Brandy snorted. "I've seen his secretary, Amanda. I doubt he's dating her."

"He's not dating me, either," Amanda reminded her.

"You go out with him practically every night."

"They aren't dates," Amanda insisted. They did feel a lot like dates...except for the way they ended. Which was exactly how she wanted them to end. "We're just...pretending to be involved."

"Have you ever considered really getting involved with him?"

"Absolutely not," Amanda said firmly. She might be having a few lustful thoughts about Josh, but she had no intention of doing anything about it. "I'm just trying to finish up our Christmas shopping list." Of course, when that was done, she wouldn't be seeing him anymore. It was far too depressing a thought.

"'Our Christmas shopping list'?" Brandy said, raising an eyebrow.

"I mean, Josh's Christmas shopping list," Amanda said. "As soon as that's finished, I won't be so busy. Then I'll have a lot more time." She glanced around her apartment again and gave herself a pep talk. "Which is a good thing considering how much work we have here."

"Right," said Brandy. "Well, in the meantime maybe we should call up the temp agency and see if we can get someone to give us a hand."

"That's a great idea," Amanda agreed. "Us Christmas elves need a lot of helpers, you know."

IF AMANDA WAS HARBORING any ideas about getting involved with Josh, she changed her mind after Hank Turnbull's open house.

It was the first affair she attended with Josh that didn't involve family, and Amanda was unusually nervous about it. She changed her clothes three times, finally settling for a dark green skirt, a matching blazer, and a ruffled white blouse. "Is this all right?" she asked Josh when he came to pick her up.

"It's fine," he assured her. "Very elflike."

"That's less than reassuring," Amanda complained as he helped her on with her coat. "You know, you really should pay more attention to what people wear at these things—just so you can tell your date."

Josh shrugged that off. "I don't usually take 'dates' to these things. And I'm sure it doesn't matter what you wear. These aren't my relatives, remember? They're just business acquaintances." He grinned happily. "We don't even have to find out personal things about them. We can just relax."

"Maybe you can," Amanda muttered. "But I imagine they'll be curious about me."

She was right. Hank Turnbull and his wife were charming people, and the rest of his business acquaintances were pleasant. However, it was obvious from their questions that they were indeed curious about her, and about her relationship with Josh. After answering a number of questions, Amanda managed to escape into a corner. She was sipping on a drink and enjoying a few moments of peace and quiet when a statuesque brunette named Susan Smyth wandered over to talk to her. "I've been really curious about you," Susan confided. "I wanted to meet the woman who finally captured Josh Larkland's attention." Her lips moved into a friendly, teasing smile. "What did you have to do? Hit him over the head with a sledge-hammer?"

"Not exactly," Amanda murmured. She glanced across the room at Josh. "Although sometimes I've been tempted."

"I know what you mean." Susan eyed Josh over Amanda's shoulder. "I...uh...went out with him a few times, you know. He's a remarkably compelling man, isn't he?"

Amanda didn't want to think about how attractive Josh was. "Yes."

"Unfortunately he's the champion of all workaholics, isn't he?" Susan chatted on. "I pretty much had to force him to go out with me in the first place." She eyed Amanda with outright curiosity. "Is that how it happened with you?"

"Not exactly," Amanda murmured. She had blackmailed Josh into going out with her...but he was the one who kept forcing the issue.

"And he never called," said Susan. "I mean...never. I was always calling him."

"You were?" Amanda seldom called Josh. He always seemed to be phoning her. Sometimes she wished he'd stop doing it. Every time she talked to him on the phone her mind went blank and it took her a good ten minutes to settle down after she hung up.

"He was always late for appointments, too...or else he'd forget about them." Susan sighed. "After a while it just petered out. I got tired of chasing him, and he didn't seem interested and..." She shrugged. "Sometimes I felt as if he'd actually forgotten I existed."

"Really?" Amanda eyed Susan's perfectly put-together figure. Heavens, the woman even had a bust-line. And Josh...forgot about her?

She took another swallow of her drink, more convinced than ever that getting involved with Josh Larkland would be a very bad idea.

ALTHOUGH SHE WAS JUST pretending to be involved with Josh, Amanda discovered at Josh's cousin Alaina's that the line between pretense and reality was becoming a little blurry.

Alaina was the only one of Josh's relations Amanda was having problems liking. She was a middle-aged woman with perfectly coiffed hair, piercing blue eyes and a manner that set Amanda's teeth on edge. When she first met Amanda, she said, "I was so amazed to hear about you and Josh. Just astounded actually." She eyed Amanda up and down. "It's actually like the tenth wonder of the world." Amanda wasn't sure what she was more surprised at—the fact that Josh could get a date, or that the date was Amanda.

Josh wasn't fond of her, either. "I think I already know something personal about Alaina," he told Amanda. "She's a pain in the neck."

Unfortunately, he was right. Alaina had a professionally decorated house, which she insisted on showing to Amanda, and an extensive art collection, which she insisted on describing to Amanda.

Amanda was plotting her escape when she glanced over Alaina's shoulder and noticed Josh heavily involved in a conversation with a tall, well-proportioned redhead. Alaina's friend, Samantha, Amanda remembered. She did a quick mental run-through of her Christmas list. Sure enough, there weren't any well-built redheads on it.

"And this is a Sudcliff," Alaina advised, gesturing at one of the paintings hanging on the wall. "Isn't it fabulous?"

"Fabulous," Amanda agreed. She kept her eye on the redhead. Josh had his hands in his pockets now. The redhead was leaning forward.

She gave her own head a shake, and tried to focus on what Alaina was saying.

"I just love its primeval qualities," Alaina continued. "Don't you?"

"Yes," Amanda said in a distracted fashion. Was he smiling at that woman? He was…that slow, sexy smile that always made Amanda forget what they were talking about. She felt an overpowering and very un-Christmassy urge to smack both the redhead and Josh.

Believe it or not, Amanda was jealous, which was totally irrational. It wasn't as if she and Josh were really involved. She was here as a business associate, nothing more. So why was she consumed with jealousy by Josh's conversation with that, that...redheaded vixen?

"Is something the matter?" asked Alaina. "I thought you would be fascinated by Sudcliff's originality."

Amanda realized Alaina was eyeing her curiously, and pasted a fake smile on her face. "I'm...enthralled," she lied.

However, when they stopped at a coffee shop on the way home, she was still feeling a little put out with both Josh and his cousin. So when Josh asked, "Did you find out anything personal about Alaina?" Amanda snapped, "No, I did not, except that she's a pain in the neck."

"I told you that," Josh agreed. His eyes sparkled. "What do you say we get her a book on how the pretentious really live. Or would that be too personal?"

"I think it would." Amanda waited for a moment. "How about you? Do you have a brilliant gift idea for her?" She narrowed her eyes. "Or were you too busy finding out something personal about Samantha?"

"Samantha?" Josh looked blank. "Who is Samantha?"

Amanda's spirits lifted. At least she didn't stand out in his mind. "She's the woman you were talking with—you know, the redhead."

"Oh, her." Josh shrugged. "I was wondering who she was." He rolled his eyes. "The only thing personal I found out about her is that she is the most boring woman I have ever met. She's an artist of some sort. She kept talking about the surreal aspects of deep-sea diving or something of that nature. I wasn't really paying attention.''

"Good,'' Amanda murmured under her breath.

Josh leaned his elbows on the table and took a sip of his coffee. "You know, I think she was the woman Alaina was trying to set me up with.''

"Really?''

"Uh-huh.'' He smiled across the table at Amanda. "Thank goodness I've got a Christmas elf around, or I'd probably have had to go out with her.''

Amanda suddenly felt better. Then she was annoyed with herself for feeling better.

This Christmas elf stuff was starting to drive her crazy.

8

"DON'T TELL ME, let me guess," Mable said when Josh walked passed her desk a couple of days later. "You are leaving early. Again."

"Uh-huh," Josh said.

"Another family party?"

"Uh-huh."

Mable eyed him thoughtfully. "You know, for someone who hated going to family get-togethers, you're sure going to a lot of them."

Josh shrugged. "I'm just giving Amanda a hand."

"Really?" Mable's eyes twinkled. "I don't know, Josh. It almost seems as if you're starting to enjoy them."

"I think I might be," Josh said thoughtfully. He shoved his hands into his pockets and strode out the door. Mable was right. He was enjoying these parties a lot more than he used to. Of course, that was because he had Amanda. He had no idea how he'd ever coped without her.

Over the past weeks he'd discovered a lot of great things about having his very own Christmas elf. The "I'll have to check with Amanda" excuse was one of them. It was a wonderful way of getting out of things he didn't want to do without getting anyone mad at him.

He enjoyed using it, too. He liked the way it felt

to be part of a couple—that there was another person who was involved in his schedule outside of work. And it was the truth. He always checked with Amanda. She had easily and seemingly effortlessly taken over all the mundane details of his social life. She handled his relatives. She took care of the invitations, and thought up wonderful reasons for refusing.

They didn't refuse that many. In spite of his token objections, and the chance of being fed something he didn't like, Josh looked forward to attending family gatherings. For a long time, he'd felt as if his relatives lived in an alien world that he wasn't a part of. Now he felt like he was becoming part of it again. He'd forgotten how much he liked most of his family, and he was becoming increasingly fascinated by finding out personal things about them.

That wasn't the only reason he enjoyed those parties. Probably the biggest reason was Amanda. He looked forward to the time they spent together. It wasn't like being with other women, where he had to make an effort at conversation and usually pretend an interest he didn't feel in what they were saying. He never felt that way with Amanda. He enjoyed everything about her...except the way she scampered out of his car when he took her home. He was finding that increasingly frustrating.

He'd told himself that a business relationship with Amanda was fine with him. However, he was starting to think that an exclusively business relationship was the last thing he wanted with his Christmas elf.

"DO WE HAVE ANYTHING on that Christmas list for Tom yet?" Josh asked Amanda as they drove to Louise and Franks's place later.

Amanda did a quick mental run-through of her list. "No, we don't. Why?"

"Marilla gave me the title of a book he wants. It's a Hungarian philosophy book. I don't know if that's personal, but..."

"It'll do," said Amanda. She waited for a moment. "You saw Marilla today?"

"Uh-huh. I dropped by her office to take her to lunch."

Amanda stared at him. "You did?"

"Yes, I did." He slowed for a light. "She's my sister, Amanda. I should know where she works." He was silent for a moment. "She also asked me what I thought she should get you for Christmas."

"Oh, no," Amanda said. She hadn't thought of his family wanting to exchange presents with her. "I don't want..."

"You never told me you could do that," Josh accused. "I thought you had to be subtle about this. I didn't know you could just ask someone what they wanted!"

"You can't just ask! However, it's all right to ask one of the couple if they have any suggestions for the other."

"Okay," Josh said. "In that case you'd better tell me what you want so I can pass it on."

"I don't want anything," Amanda said. "You can't let your family get me presents, Josh. You just can't."

"Why not?" Josh asked, his familiar puzzled-looking expression on his face.

"Because you can't. The only reason they'd get me presents is because they think you and I are involved in a relationship and we aren't!"

"Sure we are," said Josh comfortably. "You're my elf. Isn't that a relationship?"

"It's not the one they have in mind," Amanda said. "I'm serious about this. I don't want presents from your family. I'd feel terribly guilty about it. Just tell them that I don't feel I know them well enough to exchange presents with them."

Josh started to argue, then, taking one look at her face, he held up a hand. "All right. I'll tell them. But what do you want, by the way?"

"Josh!"

"I'm just curious, that's all. What does an elf want for Christmas? Besides an office, I mean."

"An office?" Amanda repeated.

"Well, you could certainly use something," Josh explained. "Your apartment seems to get smaller and more cluttered every time I pick you up."

Amanda was touched that he'd noticed. "You're right, it does. My apartment was fine as a make-do office when we didn't have much business. But now that we have business, it's not big enough. We've also hired a couple of temps to help out, so there always seem to be people around. Sometimes I can't even find a private place to change my clothes."

"You can change your clothes at my place if you like." He glanced over, grinning. "After all, we are supposed to be living together."

Amanda imagined herself undressing in his place and shivered. *Steady Amanda, steady. You don't want to get involved, remember?* "Thank you, but I'll manage somehow."

"Why don't you just rent yourself an office?" Josh asked after a moment.

"We can't afford it right now. But someday we're

going to." Amanda closed her eyes and pictured it. "Someday I'm going to have an office with my name on the door. Permanent. So you can't erase it." She chuckled. "I've been downsized, and right-sized, and then I was a temp. It's no fun. You just get attached to something and they take it away. That's why I'm doing this. I want my very own office with my very own name carved on the door, so the only person who can kick me out is me." She hesitated. "And it's not going to have the word elf anywhere on it, either."

IT WAS JOSH'S IDEA to go to Charmaine's cosmic connection meeting. "She's my sister," he'd explained. "I think I should know what weird thing she's into."

Charmaine was clearly delighted they'd come.

She led them around her beige and green living room, introducing her to the other guests, who, Amanda was amused to discover, mostly did seem to be from Detroit. Then she proudly showed them a large crystal pyramid that was sitting in the middle of the dark oak coffee table. "For meditation later," she explained.

Josh's eyes widened and for a moment Amanda was afraid he was going to announce she had another headache. Instead he produced a heroic smile, said "I'm looking forward to that," and wandered over to check out the buffet.

Charmaine turned to Amanda. "I'm so thrilled about you and Josh," she confided. "I can just feel the connection between you two."

"Can you?" Amanda glanced across the room, where Josh was heavily involved in studying the food. He caught her eye, grinned and mouthed "No fish" before turning away. She could almost feel the connection herself.

"Josh and I used to be connected, too," said Charmaine. "In a platonic way, of course. When we were younger, we were very close."

"You were?" Amanda had a hard time imagining that. There was something so otherworldly about Josh's gorgeous stepsister that she couldn't imagine her having much in common with Josh.

"Yes." Charmaine's dark eyes lit up with mirth. "I used to get into terrible trouble because of him. He could talk me into almost anything. It would be his idea, and I'd get the blame."

"I can believe that," Amanda murmured.

"Oh, and he was always doing the most dreadful things to my boyfriends. I don't think there was one he liked. He'd wire up their car so the horn wouldn't stop. And he once set up some kind of system so when my date walked me to the door, this deep voice said, 'Touch her and you will be liquidated' over and over." She rolled her eyes. "You can imagine what that did for my social life."

"Not a whole lot?" Amanda said, with a smile.

When Charmaine went to greet some guests who had just arrived, Amanda chatted with Edwina, Marilla and Shelby. There weren't many other relatives present. "Not many of us can understand Charmaine," Shelby explained tactfully. "However, Marilla and I always come. After all, Charmaine is our sister. If it's important to her, it's important to us. I hope you can persuade Josh to come to a few more...for moral support."

But I won't be here, Amanda thought. And it

wasn't just Josh she was going to miss. It was his entire family, as well.

She was just pondering this depressing thought when a smooth young man dressed entirely in beige came up to her. "Hi," he said. "Maurice. From Detroit." He rested an outstretched arm against the wall and looked down at her with obvious admiration. "I don't believe I've seen you around here before."

"I wouldn't think so," Amanda said. Was it her imagination or was this guy coming on to her? "I'm Amanda," she said. "From…the North Pole."

"Perhaps I ran into you there, during one of my cosmic journeys," Maurice suggested. He looked deeply into her eyes. "Don't you feel that we've met on another plane?" He took her hand and squeezed it tight.

"Not really," Amanda said. "Actually, I'm… uh…a little afraid of flying, so I usually take the bus." She tried to extract her hand and failed. She glanced over her shoulder. Josh was deeply involved in his discussion with Charmaine, and Shelby and Marilla had joined him. Amanda heaved a mental sigh. She'd wanted him to communicate with his family. She just wished right now he'd communicate with her.

She focused back on Maurice and gave him a tentative smile. "Well, it's been great talking to you, but I really should…"

"It's wonderful talking to you, too," Maurice said. "But words aren't necessary between connected individual minds. Don't you feel the same way?"

She was certainly feeling something. "You're so right about that," said Amanda. "Will you excuse me, please? I have to go check on Josh. I have a feeling he's getting a terrible headache.''

"THAT WAS CERTAINLY an experience," Amanda said as they left Charmaine's party a few hours later.

"It was certainly something." Josh made a face. "And I seemed to have missed the point. Why were we sitting there in the dark, staring at that plastic pyramid?"

"I think it was a crystal pyramid," said Amanda, hiding her smile. "We were supposed to be getting in touch with our inner self to form a cosmic connection to the universe. You seemed to be getting right into it."

"I wasn't," Josh grumbled. "I was trying to figure out how I could wire up the thing."

"Wire it up?"

"So it would say something. Just imagine the expression on all those people's faces if that plastic pyramid had made a sudden announcement. Something like 'Josh Larkland, you left your lights on.'" He chuckled. "That would have cleared the room in a hurry and given us an excuse to leave."

Amanda laughed along with him. "I guess it was a rather bizarre experience."

"Bizarre isn't the word." He stepped on the gas a little too hard. "Some of those people were more than a little off-the-wall. One of them kept asking me how I was feeling."

"Oh, him." Amanda chuckled. "That's because I told him I felt you had a headache coming on. It was the only excuse I could think of to get away from him."

Josh scowled. "Get away from him?"

"Yes. He was trying to cosmically connect with me."

"He was, was he?" Josh's expression darkened. "Well, he can forget that." He stopped at a red light and locked gazes with her. "If anyone is going to cosmically connect with you, it's going to be me."

His strong, possessive tone and the expression in his dark eyes warmed Amanda from head to toe. Then he swiveled his head to face the front. "After all, you are my elf."

Right, thought Amanda. The elf you hired. For a second there she'd thought he might be a little jealous. "What did you think of Charmaine's boyfriend?" she asked after a moment.

Josh gave her a puzzled look. "Boyfriend? You mean Charmaine's *dating* one of those guys?"

"Well, yes, she is."

Josh looked totally flummoxed by that. "Which one?"

"Russell."

"Oh?" He blinked. "Which one was Russell? The one with Saturn tattooed on his cheek, or the one with the diamond in his left nostril?"

"I think it was the diamond."

"Oh." He scowled. "Well, I don't like it. I don't think Charmaine should be dating a forty-year-old guy who doesn't have a decent job."

Amanda stared at him. "How do you know so much about him?"

"I asked him," said Josh. "There wasn't anything else to talk about and I was getting tired of staring at that pyramid so I asked him how old he was and what he did for a living just to pass the time." He smiled fleetingly. "It's a great way to start a conversation."

"That's...true, I suppose," Amanda agreed, making a valiant attempt not to laugh.

"It wasn't a great conversation," Josh continued. "He said he thought gainful employment was for people who couldn't find contentment in their universe! It took me half the night to figure out that meant he doesn't have a job." He lowered his brow. "Of course, I shouldn't be all that surprised. Charmaine always attracts losers."

"Really?" Amanda said, surprised that he remembered.

"Uh-huh. Even when we were kids, I was always having to scare them off." He chuckled. "And you wouldn't believe some of the things I had to do." He was silent for a moment. When he looked over at her, his eyes glinted with mischief. "You know, Amanda. I think I've just thought up the perfect present for Charmaine."

Amanda eyed him suspiciously. "If it's got anything to do with wiring up her house so it *talks* to her dates, you can forget it." She paused. "Although I must admit, it would be extremely personal."

"YOU HAVE GOT TO DO something about this apartment," Josh complained a few days later.

He sat in her kitchen, his feet propped up on one of her chairs, and shook his head at the stacks of papers and boxes in the living room. "There isn't room to swing a cat, much less an elf."

"I know," said Amanda. "But it will soon be over." It would, too. There was just over a week before Christmas. Josh was picking her up to go to his mother's open house, and had come early so they could go through a status report.

"I hope I'm going to be ready on time." He stretched back and closed his eyes. "Okay. Let's go through this gift list."

Amanda obediently began reading from her notes. "We've got the Halsone for Mimi, fishing tackle for Reg, and a red toothbrush holder for your aunt Judith." She hesitated. "Are you sure your aunt Judith wants a toothbrush holder?"

"Uh-huh," Josh said without opening his eyes. "I broke hers when I was six. I think it's time I replaced it. But maybe we could get her some photograph albums, as well. She needs some new ones."

Amanda studied him. "How do you know?"

"I was over there the other day to set the time on her VCR and we were looking at some photographs." He rolled his eyes. "I'm telling you, Amanda, as soon as my prototype circuitry is in production, I'm going to install a voice-activated VCR in Judith's place. She doesn't have one clue how to do it." He gestured at the list. "Go on."

"Okay. You're giving Marilla an A-12 Pneumatic Door Activator—whatever that is."

"It's an automatic sensor so their cats can open the window themselves," Josh explained. "Marilla was so worried that her cats weren't going to be able to let themselves out while she was at work. With this, they should be able to do it themselves—assuming I can get it tuned to the correct 'meow.'"

"It sounds…perfect," Amanda said. She returned to reading her list. "Shelby's getting the computer equipment, but we don't have anything for Gordon. I…"

"Yeah, we do," Josh said. "I was out at the university to see Shelby and she mentioned Gordon is into building model boats.'' He opened one eye. ''I don't know if that's personal, but…''

''It'll be fine,'' Amanda assured him. ''You had lunch with Shelby?''

''Uh-huh. I had to go to the university to check up on the equipment out there. She showed me around.'' He grinned. ''I still don't understand what she teaches, but at least now I know where she does it. Go on.''

''We've got a tie for your uncle Frank. And a pasta maker…''

''A pasta maker?'' Josh's eyes widened. ''We're not giving my mother a pasta maker. I…''

''I know,'' said Amanda. ''I thought we'd give it to Alaina.''

Josh grinned. ''Perfect.''

Amanda referred back to her notes. ''I think that's about it. We still don't have anything for your mother yet, but I did find a crystal moon pendant for Charmaine.''

''I think my idea was much better.'' Josh stroked his finger across his bottom lip. ''You know, Amanda, I really don't like the idea of her dating weird men with tattoos on their cheek.''

''Don't you?'' Amanda watched his finger, then dragged her gaze back to her notes. She must have a serious problem if a man's finger turned her on.

Josh didn't seem to be suffering from the same problem. ''What I'd really like to get her is a decent man with a decent job. Every time I think of that Russell character I get cold shivers.''

''Do you?'' said Amanda. Every time she thought of him she got hot shivers—for an entirely different reason.

"You know who she should meet? She should meet Wendell."

"Wendell?" Amanda echoed absently.

"Wendell Philmore. He's one of the techs who works for me. He's a little peculiar, too—but he's not a bad guy. He's certainly much better than that Russell character. At least he's got a job in this universe."

Amanda gaped at him. "Are you actually thinking of setting up your own sister with somebody?"

"Why not?" said Josh. "Everyone does it to me. Besides, who knows? Maybe Charmaine and Wendell will cosmically connect."

It was possible, and Amanda was thrilled he was this interested in his sister's life. "Maybe they will."

"Good. Why don't you arrange it?"

"Arrange what?"

"Having them over," Josh prompted. "That's how everyone always sets me up."

"Having them over," Amanda repeated slowly. "You mean, to your place?"

"Uh-huh. Oh, and don't just have them. We might as well have everyone we don't have a present for. That way we can quiz them without having to go anywhere. Be sure to include my mother—she hasn't seen my place for a while." He tapped his fingers on his thigh, obviously taken with the idea. "Oh, and we might as well ask my other sisters, too. From the way they talk, I sometimes wonder if they have any idea about what I do."

"They don't, but…"

"They can see it at my place. I've got most of my prototype equipment there. Oh, I think Uncle Reg would be interested in that, as well, so we should ask him, too." He looked over at Amanda. "You can do this, can't you?"

"Well...uh...I suppose, but..."

"Good," said Josh. "How about tomorrow?"

9

JOSH WAS IN the process of packing up his things when Mable came into his office. "I know," she said before he could say anything. "You're leaving early."

"Uh-huh," he said. "I have to get right home. There's something wrong with my microwave." He liked the way that sounded. He'd often been around when other men had been summoned home to fix some emergency. They'd always rolled their eyes and looked exasperated, but they'd looked a little pleased, as well. Josh had never understood why, but now he did. He liked the feeling that someone not connected with work needed his help.

Mable looked down at the phone, then back at him. "Your microwave *phoned* you?" She shook her head. "This high-tech stuff is getting so it's beyond me."

"My microwave didn't phone me, although that's a great idea," Josh explained. "Amanda phoned me. She's trying to get the microwave to work, but when she tries to turn it on, the oven cuts in."

"Amanda's at your place?"

"Uh-huh." The image of her in his place gave him a pleasant thrill. "We're having a few people over tonight." He liked saying that, too. It was exactly the sort of thing a couple did—have people over to their place. He was looking forward to it, too. He wanted to show his family what he did, and he was eager to see their reaction.

Mable's eyes widened considerably. *"You?"*

"Yeah, me." He frowned. "I wanted to do it last night, but Amanda insisted she needed more than one day's notice to organize it. She gets funny about things like that sometimes."

"How…peculiar." Mable eyed him suspiciously. "It's not a Christmas party, is it?"

"Not really," he said, although now that she'd mentioned it, it was sort of a Christmas party. "I guess you could say we're having a few people over under the umbrella of a Christmas theme."

"Good heavens," Mable said faintly. "Is there…uh…going to be singing?"

"There better not be," Josh said.

"Good," Mable said. "At least I know one thing hasn't changed."

Josh had a condo in an upscale area of Calgary. He'd chosen it because of the location, had it professionally decorated, professionally cleaned, and, apart from sleeping there, he spent less than ten hours a week in the place. When he wasn't in it, he'd be hard-pressed to describe what his apartment looked like.

However, when he let himself in at six-o'clock, he knew immediately that it didn't usually look or smell like this.

He noticed the scent as soon as he stepped inside— a Christmassy mixture of pine intermingled with delicious food odors wafting from the kitchen. "Amanda?" he called.

Amanda came out of the kitchen. She stopped in the doorway and stared at him with obvious surprise.

"Oh," she said. "I didn't expect you to be here this early."

Josh took one look at her and felt as if he'd just been hit in the solar plexus. She had on another one of her bright red dresses, her short blond hair curled damply around her ears, her face was flushed and she wasn't wearing any shoes. She looked sweet, and sexy, and desirable. Just seeing her looking like that, in his place, was an incredible turn-on.

"You didn't have to rush home just because I couldn't get the microwave to work," Amanda continued. "I could have coped for a little while."

Josh cleared his throat. "I...uh...thought I'd better," he explained. He kicked off his boots and hung his coat in the closet. "Besides, I was planning on coming home anyway to give you a hand."

"Really?" She smiled and her eyes sparkled with appreciation. "Well, that was very nice of you."

"Very nice" wasn't a good description for him right now, Josh thought. "Decidedly lustful" was. He gave his head a shake to clear it and took a look around, not all that surprised to see a fully decorated Christmas tree in one corner of the living room. There was a fire in the fireplace, the furniture had been polished to a shine, and everything looked clean and fresh and homey. "Not that it looks like you need a hand."

"Just with the oven," said Amanda. "And it is working. It just won't...mind its own business." She furrowed her brow. "I just hope I haven't broken something. I'm not used to working with such smart appliances."

"You can't break anything," Josh assured her. He

put an arm across her shoulders, getting another rush from touching her. "Let's take a look."

Amanda stood beside him as he checked the sensitivity circuitry on the microwave. Her scent surrounded him, making it difficult for him to concentrate, so it took him longer than it should have to make the adjustments. "Now I know why there aren't a lot of elves in high-tech industries," he said as he turned to face her.

She tilted up her head, looking puzzled. "Why?"

"It's too distracting." He took a step toward her. "Dim lights," he said. The lights dimmed. The microwave didn't come on.

"I think you fixed it," said Amanda, and she looked impressed.

"It's because of the prototype circuit board," Josh said. "I had to improvise here. When the new houses are built, they'll have things set up properly. Then we won't have these sorts of problems."

"Oh," Amanda said. Her tongue flicked across her bottom lip. "Are you going to move into one of those new homes?"

Josh seldom gave one second of thought to where he lived now, much less where he might live in the future, and right now he didn't care, as long as she was going to be in the kitchen. "I might," he said.

"Oh," she said again.

Her gaze met his. Her eyes were a deeper shade of green than he'd seen them before, the blush on her cheeks a darker pink, and her breathing was faster than normal. Was that a reaction to him being so close? Josh's own breathing rate increased at the idea that it was. He toyed with the idea of pressing his lips against the smooth skin of her throat to see what her reaction would be to that. However, before he could do it, Amanda took a wary step backward. "We've got less than an hour before people start arriving," she said briskly. "If you're going to take a shower, you should probably do it now."

Maybe she'd like to join him. Josh considered inviting her, but something in her eyes told him now was not a good time. "Good idea," he said instead.

He wandered up the stairs and into the bathroom. Amanda's shampoo and perfume and hair-dryer were lying on the counter. The towels from her shower were damp, and held a lingering scent of her. The idea of her standing totally naked in his shower was even more arousing than her bare feet. Too bad his shower wasn't a smart appliance. He'd like to know what it had to say about her naked body. No, actually, he'd rather find out for himself.

There was no doubt about it. He wanted to do something with his Christmas elf that had nothing to do with business arrangements...or Christmas.

A BUSINESS FUNCTION, Amanda reminded herself as she studied the buffet. This was a business function; she was catering a business function and Josh Larkland was nothing more than her employer at a business function.

But when Josh came padding into the dining room a few minutes later, the term "business function" fled from her brain, along with almost everything else. He was wearing a pair of brown pants, his pale yellow shirt was unbuttoned and he was clutching his socks in his right hand. The man even had sexy toes, not to mention the great wide, muscular chest that went with everything else that was great about him. "This looks terrific,'' he approved as he surveyed the food. ''Did you do it all?''

Clean men, Amanda was thinking. There's something so appealing about a clean man. In all honesty, though, she'd probably find Josh appealing if he were covered with mud.

She grinned at the image and ordered her brain to clear. ''Just me, the caterers, the cleaners and almost everyone else in the city. You know, Josh, the next time you plan a party, you should do it with more than forty-eight hours' notice. It would be a lot easier—and a lot cheaper.''

''I don't plan on having another party,'' he said. ''I don't even think I planned this party.'' That familiar puzzled look crept over his face. ''As a matter of fact, I didn't even realize it *was* a party until Mable told me. I thought we were just having a few people over.''

Only Josh would be that clued out. ''When it's your entire family, it's a party! The amazing thing is that they're almost all coming, too, in spite of the short notice. Mimi canceled tickets to the theater, Francine and Wally are missing Wally's office party, and Charmaine is forgoing the New Moon Avizandum so she could come.''

''Great. We want Charmaine here so she can meet Wendell. Maybe she'll cosmically connect with him and forget the other bozos.'' He studied the buffet table. ''The good news is, there is enough food here for a few hundred people—and I know for sure none of it has anything to do with fish.'' He gave Amanda a warning look. ''It doesn't, does it?''

''No, of course not.''

''Good thing.'' He turned to face her. ''Now, what

can I do to help? It has to be something technical. I'm no good with knives, cutting things up, setting things out, cooking things or cleaning things up.'' He smiled his slow, sexy smile. "But I've got lots of talent in other areas.''

Did he mean what she thought he meant? Probably not. "Good,'' she said. "Then how about demonstrating them by putting on some music? The stereo refuses to listen to me.''

Josh leaned against the wall while he pulled on his socks. "That's because the stereo is not modified for voice input yet. All you have to do is press the On button.''

"I never thought of that,'' Amanda said, smiling. As Josh walked around with a loose, easy, yet sexy stride, she kept reminding herself that this party was business, strictly business. But it was near impossible to keep her mind on business when Josh was tantalizingly near, so she fled into the kitchen.

She was taking the vegetable tray out of the fridge when the sounds of Christmas music filled the condo. Josh came into the kitchen. "How's that?''

"Good. Thank you.''

"You're welcome. Say, where did I get that collection of Christmas music? I didn't think I had any.''

"You didn't,'' Amanda said. "I brought it with me.''

"What about the tree? Did you bring that with you, too?''

"No. That I had delivered.''

His forehead wrinkled. "I didn't know you could have a tree delivered—complete with ornaments and strings of lights.''

"You can have almost anything delivered, as long

as you're willing to pay for it,'' Amanda informed him. ''This is not going to be a cheap party, Josh. There's the food, the cleaners, the caterers… Oh, and I also had to buy Christmas ornaments because you didn't have any.''

Josh shrugged. ''I never needed them before.'' He put his head to one side. ''You think of everything, don't you?''

''That's why us elves are paid the big bucks,'' Amanda quipped. ''We're supposed to think of everything.''

''Ah,'' said Josh. ''Well, you're very good at it.''

There was a gleam in his eye that hadn't been there before. Amanda's heart rate increased. She bent her head and busied herself with the vegetables. ''I like doing it. And it's fun working in your kitchen—when the appliances cooperate, that is.''

''Is it?'' Josh shrugged. ''I wouldn't know. I don't cook here much. As a matter of fact, no one cooks here much.''

''I gathered that from the dust in the oven.'' Amanda glanced over her shoulder at him. ''You must have had other women in here to cook you a meal?''

''Nope.'' He examined the bottles of wine sitting on the counter. ''Should I open these?''

''Yes. You mean…never?''

''No,'' said Josh. ''Never. At least, not that I can remember.''

''Why not?''

He shrugged as if it wasn't important. ''I don't know.'' He finished opening the wine, and rounded the corner to stand behind her.

''You must have people over sometime,'' Amanda persisted.

"Just some guys." He was so close she could feel his breath against her neck. "You know, a bunch of propeller-heads talking techy-byte stuff, drinking beer and eating pretzels."

The doorbell rang as Amanda was setting out the vegetable tray. She straightened her dress, whisked off her apron, and found her shoes. "How do I look?"

She expected him to say "elflike" or something of that nature. Instead he said, "I think you're missing something." Then he stepped forward, put his arms around her and before Amanda realized what was happening, he was kissing her—a hard, hot kiss that started with his mouth stroking over hers, then his tongue licking along her top lip, moving around to her bottom lip, then sliding inside her mouth. His body was hard against hers, her breasts crushed against his chest and Amanda couldn't think of anything except how good it felt, and how much she wished it would go on forever.

But it didn't. The doorbell rang again. "I suppose one of us better get that," Josh mumbled against her lips.

He released her, and stepped back. Amanda blinked up at him, her mind still numb from his kiss. "Just a minute," she said as he started to move toward the door. "You've got lipstick…"

"That's okay." He grinned. "Now we both look as if we live together."

IT WAS ONE O'CLOCK in the morning when Amanda and Josh bade goodbye to the last of their guests and collapsed onto the couch, with the enthusiastic comments from Josh's family still ringing in their ears.

"It was fabulous, Amanda. However, I would add a dash of cinnamon to the veggie dip. It gives it such flavor."

"A Siamese would be perfect here, Amanda. And it could even let itself out!"

"Wonderful gadgets, Josh. I had no idea they used these sorts of things on trains." And, obscurely, from Aunt Judith, "What an amazing bathroom, dear. The sink is so...white!"

Edwina and Harold were the last to leave. Edwina had given Amanda an extra-long hug just before she went out. "Thank you so much, Amanda," she'd said, and Amanda knew she wasn't just thanking her for the evening.

Josh rubbed an eye and yawned. "That's the problem with having your own party," he groaned. "You can't leave when you feel like it."

Which was probably a good thing, thought Amanda. If they'd been somewhere else, she probably would have dragged him out the door after that mind-numbing kiss in the kitchen. She'd spent half the evening trying not to think about it, and the other half thinking about it anyway. And every time she'd looked at him, she'd thought about it again.

She looked up at him. His head was back against the pillows, his eyes were half closed and a small smile of satisfaction played across his lips. "You don't look like someone who wanted to leave," she accused. "You look like someone who had a good time."

His lips curved upward. "Yeah, I guess I did. Except when Uncle Frank started reciting actuarial tables to me." He dropped a casual arm around her shoulders. "He had on that same ugly blue tie, too. It's a good thing we got him a new one."

"Uh-huh." Amanda rested her head against his shoulder. "What about your mother? Did you have any brilliant ideas for her yet?"

"No." He sighed, then brightened. "But I did come up with something for Aunt Francine."

Amanda glanced up at him. "You did?"

"Yup." Josh sounded smug. "She wants a variable speed, battery-operated reversible drill."

Amanda tried to imagine the proper-looking Francine with a variable-speed drill and failed completely. "Are you sure?"

"Absolutely positive. She kept playing with mine." He chuckled. "Although I'm not too sure she knew what it was. It didn't look as if Wendell and Charmaine hit it off, after all. They hardly said a word to each other all evening."

"I think they were connecting," Amanda told him. "And they did leave together."

"Good." He stretched back, his lips widening into a smile. "Did you see Aunt Mimi and Uncle Reg? They spent the entire evening wandering from room to room saying 'lights on, lights off.'"

"They were impressed," Amanda said. "Your whole family was impressed, Josh. You should have shown them all this years ago."

"I never thought about it." He shifted sideways so he was facing her, and raised a hand to brush a strand of hair off her cheek. "What I should have done is gotten a Christmas elf years ago."

His palm moved across her face, and he ran his thumb along her bottom lip. Amanda could hear her own heartbeat, feel herself gasping with pleasure at his touch. Then his mouth was where his thumb used to be, hot and heavy against hers, while his tongue curled around hers and his hands pulled her closer. This was strictly a business function, Amanda reminded herself hazily, but it was impossible to think about business functions when his large palms were gently stroking down her back.

He slid back, taking her with him, so his head rested against the arm of the sofa, still kissing her, his arms wrapped around her. When they finally came up for air, Amanda was sprawled on top of him, her legs entwined with his, her hips pressed against his. The heat emanated from him, and the knowledge that he wanted her as much as she wanted him increased her desire.

She raised her head. His face was ruddy, his eyelids drooping sensuously, and his breathing was as rapid and uneven as her own. "We shouldn't be doing this," she said, having trouble catching her breath. "This is supposed to be a business relationship, remember? I'm just your Christmas elf and..."

"I know," Josh said. "But I've never made love with an elf before." His hand moved up and down her back. "Do you really think it's an experience I should miss?"

Amanda hesitated. If she refused, he wouldn't make a fuss about it. He'd just say something like "Too bad" and never mention it again.

But he was right underneath her. She could feel his hardness and she could see the passion in his eyes. She didn't want to refuse. Right now, she just wanted him. "I don't think it's an experience you should miss, either," she whispered.

"Good," said Josh. He eased her head back down

to his. "Because that's all I could think about all evening."

Then he was kissing her again, holding her hips
against his so she could feel him against her, and even
though they were dressed, the sensation was so erotic
and so arousing that Amanda moaned and bit against
his neck, squirming against him to get closer. He fumbled with the zipper on her dress, finally raising his
head so he could see what he was doing. "That's
going to be my next invention," he growled into her
ear. "A voice-activated zipper." The feel of his
breath, the knowledge that he was as aroused as she
was, excited Amanda even more.

He finally got it undone, and raised her up into a
sitting position so he could work the dress off her
shoulders and down to her waist. His hands trembled
slightly and when he freed her breasts from her bra
his eyes widened and his lips curled into his slow,
sexy smile. He cupped a breast in each hand, and
rubbed his thumb across her nipples. Amanda gasped
with pleasure and his eyes darkened. "You like
that?" he asked.

"Yes," Amanda breathed.

"So do I."

He fondled her breasts while she undid his shirt.
When she pressed her palms against his warm, bare
chest, he closed his eyes and groaned and pulled her
down so he could take a breast in his mouth. Amanda
was so mindless with pleasure that she only half realized he was trying to remove the rest of her clothes
until he raised her up a little. "We have to move,
Amanda," he mumbled against her skin. "I'm no
good at undressing someone on a sofa."

He eased her up, but instead of taking her to his

bedroom, as she expected, he slid down to the floor, taking her with him. "I want to do this here, beside the Christmas tree," he explained. "It seems rather…fitting."

Amanda didn't care where they did it as long as it happened right now. She helped him get her clothes off, laughing as he complained about her panty hose—"I have no idea how you women get these things on"—then, seeing the expression on his face as he looked at her, she didn't feel like laughing anymore.

He knelt to remove his pants, then stretched down beside her, pulling her against his naked body, easing his thigh between her legs, then gently parting her and sliding a finger into her. Amanda arched against him. He took her breast in his mouth again, caressing a nipple with his tongue, while his fingers searched and found the sensitive place between her legs. He kept moving his fingers and touching her and licking her breasts as the pressure built inside Amanda, finally driving her over the edge into a shuddering climax.

Then Josh was rolling away from her to pull a condom out of his pants' pocket. "Just a little planning ahead," he explained, catching the surprised look on her face. He used his teeth to rip open the foil packet. "I told you. I've been thinking about this all evening."

Then he pulled her down onto him, parting her, easing himself up into her. "Oh, Amanda," he groaned into her ear, as he wrapped his arms around her. They moved together, at first slowly, then faster and harder and deeper, and Amanda moaned her pleasure into his ear.

Afterward, they cuddled together on his carpet, with the Christmas tree lights pulsing down on them. "I liked that," Josh announced in a satisfied-sounding voice.

"Me, too," Amanda murmured. She rested her head against his chest and closed her eyes.

"Good." He caressed a hand up and down her arm. "Let's go up to the bedroom and do it again there. And then we could try the kitchen..."

Amanda raised her head to look at his face. "Are you planning some sort of marathon here?"

"Why not?" Josh asked. He took her into his arms and smiled up at her. "After all, we've got all night."

We've got longer than that, Amanda thought. We've got until Christmas Eve.

10

"YES, I KNOW," Josh said to Mable as he walked into his office three days later. "I'm a little late, aren't I?"

"You're not just a little late," Mable scolded. "It's almost eleven." She frowned at him, although her eyes sparkled. "First you start leaving at five. Now you don't come in until eleven. What's next? Are you going to stop coming in at all?"

"I'm considering it," he said, chuckling at her expression. "It's Christmas, Mable. People have things to do at Christmas."

"Like what?"

Like spending most of the morning making love with Amanda. Josh almost blurted that out before he remembered it wasn't the sort of information Mable needed to know. "Just...things," he said. "And I'm going to be leaving early, too, so if I've got any appointments after three, you'll have to reschedule them. I'm going shopping."

"Shopping?" Mable looked more astonished than ever. "You're going shopping?"

"Uh-huh. I told Amanda I'd give her a hand." He grinned again as he recalled the way Amanda's eyes had sparkled when he'd offered to accompany her.

"Amanda, hmm?" Mable cleared her throat. "You

two sure seem to be spending a lot of time together these days.''

Josh nodded. He had been spending a lot of time with Amanda. She'd spent every night since their Christmas party at his place. When they weren't attending a family or a business function, they spent the evening together, watching television, reviewing their Christmas shopping list, talking and making love.

Josh was enjoying every second of it. It wasn't at all like any of his other brief relationships. He didn't feel obligated to spend time with Amanda. He wanted to do it. She never got annoyed with him because he forgot an appointment they'd made, because he never forgot an appointment. Most of the time he was early, because he was eager to see her. He liked going to his place and finding her there, and he liked not having to eat alone.

"With all this going on, it's a wonder we get any work done around here," said Mable.

Josh was already lining up his work for the day. "Don't worry," he said absentmindedly. "Soon it will be Christmas."

Mable paused at the doorway. "And then what?"

Josh shrugged. After Christmas he wouldn't be going to all these parties. He wouldn't be looking for presents, or trying to find out personal things about people. "Then things will get back to normal."

"And...uh...what about Amanda?" Mable pursued.

"What about her?" Josh hadn't thought that far ahead. Right now, he was enjoying having Amanda around. But somewhere in the back of his mind he knew that Amanda would drift out of his life, the same way other women had drifted away. The idea bothered him, so he pushed it to one side. Right now everything was perfect. They'd nearly completed his Christmas shopping list. His family was happy with him. And best of all, he had his evenings with Amanda.

Getting a Christmas elf was definitely the smartest thing he'd ever done.

"I'M STARTING TO FEEL as if we've got this under control," Brandy advised. "I've got the exhibitors arranged for the Internet trade show we're doing next month. We sent out the invitations for VisTech's open house. And we've got the corporate gifts for Dawson's Building Supplies." She looked down at the boxes. "Although I still don't understand why a building supply company wants to give their corporate pals books on horse breeding."

"Neither do I," Amanda murmured. Her mind wasn't on horse breeding…or even work. It was busy thinking about Josh…the way he'd looked this morning after his shower. She smiled.

Brandy leaned back against the sofa and studied her. "We've been so busy these past few days that it feels like I've hardly seen you."

"I have been busy," Amanda said. She'd been busy organizing Josh's office party, finishing the last of the shopping, wrapping presents…and when she wasn't doing that, she was with Josh.

"You certainly have been working long hours," Brandy said, with an innocent expression on her face. "Although I've been here before you just about every day." She paused. "Which is rather startling, since *you* live here."

Amanda flushed and averted her face. "That's another problem with using your apartment as your office. There's just no privacy."

"I'm you're best friend. We aren't supposed to have privacy from each other." Brandy's eyes sparkled. "I gather you and Josh don't have a 'business relationship' anymore."

"Not exactly," Amanda admitted.

"How about that!" Brandy said, flushing. "You and me in the same weekend."

Amanda saw the color on Brandy's cheek and the sparkle in her eyes and wondered if she looked the same way. "You mean, you and Harvy…"

"Finally," Brandy said, with a satisfied sigh. "Oh, we talked about it first. Endlessly, as a matter of fact. He had all these deep thoughts about not offending me, and what we meant to each other… It was really sweet. And then it was…wonderful. Of course I knew it would be. Harvy is so…sexy."

"Harvy?" Amanda pictured the short, rotund Harvy Denton. "Harvy is sexy?"

"Well, he is when you get to know him." Brandy's flush deepened. "He's really getting serious, Amanda. He's even invited me to meet his mother."

"Really?" Amanda smiled. She'd already met Josh's mother.

"Yes." Brandy got a dreamy look on her face. "You know, I think this might be the real thing."

Amanda had been too busy and too happy to dwell on the faint, niggling worry at the back of her mind. However, Brandy's words brought them to the front of it. "I wish I was so sure," she murmured.

"What do you mean? This has to be something, Amanda. You and Josh are together all the time—and you have been for most of the month."

"I know," Amanda said. She was positive Josh felt something for her. He certainly had to be attracted to her, considering how much time they spent making love. And she was sure she saw genuine affection in his eyes. "It's probably silly," she said. "But I think it's because Josh keeps referring to me as his Christmas elf."

"So?"

"I guess I started thinking of myself as that, too. All month I've been thinking that by Christmas Eve, I won't be shopping for Josh anymore, or going to parties with him anymore. That all will be ended by then. And now we're nearly at that point. Christmas is just a few days away," Amanda explained. "We've nearly finished Josh's shopping list. We've just got his mother left—and we'll see her at Francine's open house tonight. Then we have the Larkland Christmas party and then it will be Christmas Eve. And then what?"

"I think you're worried over nothing, Amanda," Brandy said in a reassuring tone. "You're not going to stop seeing Josh just because Christmas has arrived."

"I hope you're right," Amanda said, worried all the same.

"I NEVER KNEW shopping could be so exhausting," Josh complained as they were getting ready for Francine's party that evening.

He came out of the bathroom, buttoning up the collar on his shirt, and gave Amanda a kiss on the nose. "What were all those people doing there anyway?"

"Possibly Christmas shopping," Amanda teased. "Just like we were."

"Well, they should be more organized," Josh complained. "They should have finished their shopping a long time ago."

"You haven't finished your shopping yet," Amanda scolded. "And it wouldn't have taken us all day to find two things if you weren't so difficult! I told you. They don't *make* variable-speed reversible drills with *pink* handles."

"Aunt Francine needs a drill and she always wears pink."

"It doesn't matter," said Amanda. "People do not color coordinate their wardrobe to their work tools."

"Oh." He grinned, hugged her and then released her so they could finish dressing. "The good news is, we're nearly finished. We just have to think up something for my mother." He glanced over his shoulder at her. "You haven't had a brilliant idea, have you— besides a pasta maker, I mean?"

"No," Amanda admitted.

"Me, neither," Josh admitted. "I've talked to her, I've taken her for lunch, and I even asked Shelby and Charmaine for suggestions." He grimaced. "They weren't much help. Shelby thought I should get her a cookbook and Charmaine's idea was perfume. Obviously they're no better at this personal stuff than I am."

"We're running out of time," Amanda reminded him. "We'd better come up with some ideas tonight."

"I will." Josh's eyes sparkled at her. "We're getting down to the final stretch here. This is the last family party we have to go to. We're on the last present. Soon we'll just have the office Christmas party to get through."

A cold shiver traveled up Amanda's spine. Don't

be ridiculous, she scolded herself. So what if Christmas comes. You're going to stay right here and be with Josh... Still, she couldn't stop herself from asking. "What happens after that?"

Josh shrugged. "Things get back to normal." He expertly knotted his tie. "It's about time, too. The work is just piling up on my desk."

Amanda shivered again. The possibility of this wonderful thing with Josh ending seemed frighteningly possible.

It seemed even more possible when they were at Francine's that night.

"It's something of a family tradition," Edwina explained to Amanda. "Mimi has the first party of the season. Francine has the last one before Christmas. And then on Christmas Day, everyone comes to my place." She smiled at Amanda. "I never thought to ask before, but I assume you'll be joining us at Christmas. Or are you going to be with your own family?"

Amanda would have loved to be with her family, but they had so much business now, and it was so expensive to get there, that she had decided to stay here. She'd planned on spending the day with Brandy's family, although she had been expecting Edwina's invitation. She opened her mouth to accept, then changed her mind. "I'm not really sure what I'm doing," she said instead.

"You'll always be welcome with us," Edwina said. She gazed across the room, where Josh was involved in an animated discussion with his sisters. "Josh has been so different since you've become part of his life."

Everyone kept saying that. "It's so amazing to see the change in Josh since you're part of his life."

"Josh is so happy since you're part of his life."

"Josh is so cosmically aware since you're part of his life."

"I think Josh is starting to give serious consideration to getting a cat," Marilla said. "It's all because you've become part of his life."

Amanda watched Josh chat with his mother. She was part of his life, wasn't she? Or was she just his Christmas elf who was pretending to be part of his life?

Josh caught her eye and began moving through the crowd toward her, his face lit by a cheerful smile. "I've got it," he whispered into her ear. "A Christmas present for my mother."

"What?"

"A pearl necklace. She mentioned she broke the ones my father gave her. I'd like to replace it." He studied Amanda's face. "That is…personal, isn't it?"

"It's perfect," Amanda said, giving him a little hug. She was touched by his thoughtfulness.

"That's it, then," he said. "The last present." He grinned with pleasure. "We've done it, Amanda. Now we don't have to do this anymore."

He sounded happy about it. Amanda felt colder than ever.

"I THINK WE'VE GOT THIS organized," Amanda told Mable two days before the Larkland Christmas party.

She took an anxious look around the lobby of Larkland Technology Development. "I'll do a few more decorations on the day of the party but that's pretty much all there is left to do. The caterers are all lined up, I've arranged for the musicians…with no singing.

And I've had positive responses from almost everyone we asked.''

"You've done a great job," Mable murmured. "This is going to be one heck of a Christmas party."

"It better be," said Amanda. "Everyone Josh wants to impress is coming." She leaned back in her chair near Mable's desk. "I'm a little surprised at that. December twenty-third isn't a great time to be having a Christmas party."

"Everyone is coming because of Josh," Mable explained. "No matter what he does, people like him. I even like him, and that's not easy considering how difficult he is to work for." She paused. "Of course, he's been a lot easier to work for since you've been around."

Amanda blushed at the compliment. "I don't think I…"

"Yes, you did. You dragged him out of his office and into the real world. That's been good for him. And you put him back in touch with his family again. That's been good for him, too—and for them. But I'm not so sure it's been good for you."

Amanda felt a twinge of unease. "What do you mean?"

Mable's blue eyes were warm and wise. "You've fallen for him, haven't you?"

Amanda opened her mouth to deny it, then closed it and nodded.

"I thought so." Mable sighed heavily. "He is fond of you, too, Amanda. I know he is. And he needs you—right now anyway." Her eyebrows came down. "But I'm not too sure what's going to happen when Christmas is over."

Amanda swallowed a couple of times. "What do you mean?"

Mable winced. "I don't want to burst your bubble, and I don't want to be an interfering old woman, either. But I've known Josh for a long time. True, I've never seen him act like this before, but it is Christmas. Josh gets a little strange around Christmas." She smiled slightly. "Of course, it's hard to tell because he's a little strange most of the time."

"Mable…"

Mable stretched forward and put her hand over Amanda's. "What I'm trying to tell you is that this Josh—the one who is interested in you and spends time with you and wants to be with you—well, this isn't the Josh I'm used to. The one I'm used to spends most of his time at work, and doesn't think about anything but that."

Amanda had a brief flash of Susan's beautiful face as she'd told Amanda much the same thing. *He just forgot about me,* she'd said.

Mable's blue eyes were crystal clear across the table. "I just thought you should be prepared…in case that happens. It's not as if Josh is a bad person. He doesn't mean to hurt anyone, and he'd never do it on purpose. He just wouldn't know that he's doing it."

"I know," Amanda said. She gave Mable a swift smile. "You don't have to worry. I'm a Christmas elf, remember? Us elves can take care of ourselves."

"I hope so," said Mable. "Oh, and if it makes your job any easier, I should tell you that I've got my heart set on a bottle of brandy for Christmas."

AMANDA ARRIVED at Josh's place that evening feeling tired and depressed. They'd planned on spending the evening at home, but when she walked in, Josh still had his coat on. He kissed her when she came in, and Amanda clung to him extra hard. He released her and used a finger to raise her chin. "What's wrong?" he asked. "You look worn out."

Amanda was touched that he'd noticed and then annoyed with herself for being touched. "I'm just tired," she said. "It's all this rushing around. Thinking up Christmas presents. Buying Christmas presents. Organizing parties. Going to parties. And you should see my apartment. I can't even move in there." She rested her head against his chest. "Sometimes Christmas gets to me."

"Me, too," he said. "Cheer up. Soon it will be all over and things can get back to normal."

"Now there's a cheerful thought," Amanda muttered. She eyed his clothes. "I thought we were staying here tonight."

"We can't," said Josh. "There's this…business thing we should go to."

The last thing Amanda wanted to do was go anywhere. "Do we have to?" she asked.

"We really should." He patted her shoulder. "Come on. It's the last Christmas thing you'll have to come to."

Was that supposed to make her feel better? "Terrific," Amanda muttered. "The North Pole looks pretty good right now."

"We're not going to the North Pole. Hurry up. Get dressed. Let's get out of here."

His aura of suppressed excitement made Amanda want to either smack him or throw herself at his feet and beg him to assure her that Mable was wrong.

She was still mulling over Mable's warning when

Josh stopped the car. Amanda had been so lost in thought that she hadn't noticed where they were. Now she realized they were stopping in front of an office building. She glanced over at him. "Is this the right place?"

"Uh-huh." Josh grinned at her, his eyes sparkling with excitement. "Come on."

Amanda hesitated. The building looked pretty much deserted. "But…"

He ignored her objections and guided her into the elevator, and pressed the button for the second floor. "Are you sure you know where we're going?" Amanda asked as the elevator rose.

"Absolutely positive," said Josh.

The elevator opened onto a hallway. Josh used a hand on her back to guide her down it, and stopped in front of a glass door. Amanda looked up at him, then at the writing on the glass door in front of her. A&B Executive Services, it said in big block letters.

Amanda looked back at Josh. "What?"

"It's your Christmas present," Josh explained. "I would have wrapped it but it's a little hard to wrap an office."

"An office," Amanda echoed. She looked back up at him. "You got me an office?"

"Uh-huh." He grinned down at her. "I even had a voice-recognition door lock installed. It's coded for Brandy's voice and yours, too." He gestured at the door. "Go ahead. Open it."

"I can't believe this," Amanda said, thoroughly astonished and thoroughly delighted. She looked from him back to the door. "Open," she whispered. The door swung open.

"It's not huge or anything," said Josh as he led

her through the reception area. "But it's a lot bigger than your apartment."

It wasn't huge, but it was exactly the right size. There was a small foyer at the front, a storage area at the back, a large square work area, and two interior offices. It was all completely furnished, and the cupboard in the back was filled with stationery supplies. "These are from my family," Josh explained as he showed them to her. He held up a hand. "I know you said you didn't want them to give you anything but it was impossible to talk them out of it. I finally gave up and told them to give you office supplies, so they did." His forehead furrowed. "Except for Aunt Judith. She gave you a year's supply of toilet paper."

"That was very kind of them," Amanda said, her voice choked with emotion.

"Hey, you haven't seen the best part." Josh led her over to one of the interior offices and gestured at the wooden door. There, on the door, was her name— Amanda Kringleton—carved in big block letters.

"It's what you said you wanted," Josh reminded her. "An office with your name on the door. Of course, if you ever leave this place you'll have to take it with you."

"Oh, Josh," Amanda said inadequately, so touched she could hardly speak. "You...you did all this in just over a week?"

"I told you. I'm a fast worker when I make up my mind."

"You sure are," Amanda breathed. She turned and threw herself against him. "Thank you so much. I just...I can't...I..."

Josh chuckled and backed against the wall, taking her with him. "I guess you like it, huh?"

"Like it?" She took his face in her hands and kissed him hard. "I love it." She pushed herself against him, running her hands down him, feeling him harden in response.

"Good." He raised his head. "But is it...personal?"

"It certainly is," Amanda told him.

THE NEXT DAY she took Brandy over to show them their new quarters. "It's rent-free for six months," she explained to Brandy, passing on the information that Josh had told her. "If business keeps on the way it is, we shouldn't have any problem affording the rent after that."

"It's...amazing," Brandy said, as she wandered around, touching the desks and staring at the stationery. "I hope you got him something really good for Christmas."

"I did." Amanda smiled in satisfaction. "I got him a picture of his whole family. It's not exactly a surprise, since I had to get them all together to do it." She rolled her eyes. "That was a real adventure. Alaina phoned me four times to find out what everyone else was wearing. Francine insisted on showing up in pink. Judith wanted to wear red, so she said she wouldn't stand anywhere near her. Marilla wanted to bring all her cats. Luckily, Josh was cooperative." Her smile faded as she said his name.

"We sure were wrong about him," Brandy said. "Just like I was wrong about Harvy."

"I'm not so sure," Amanda said slowly.

Brandy peered at her. "Oh, no. You're not still worrying about that Christmas elf stuff, are you?"

Amanda sat down in her office chair. "As a matter of fact, I am."

"Well, don't. I'm sure Josh feels something for you. You're always together. He gave you an office…"

"Oh, he does feel something for me," Amanda agreed. "At least, he does right now. But I'm not so sure that will last. He keeps talking about how he can hardly wait until this is finished. I swear if he calls me his Christmas elf one more time, or says, 'I'll be glad when this is over so things can get back to normal,' I'm going to smack him."

"Why? People often…"

"I wasn't part of his normal," Amanda reminded her. "I was hired to do a job. Yes, we're attracted to each other, and yes, we're having a great time now. But after Christmas, he isn't going to need me anymore. And then what will happen?"

"Amanda…"

"I don't want to be dumped again," said Amanda. "It was bad enough when Dwight and Kyle decided they didn't need me anymore. I don't know that I want to hang around and watch Josh decide that he doesn't need me, either."

"You don't know that's going to happen," Brandy said, but she had an uncertain look on her face.

"I know. And maybe I am being silly. But I want to be prepared."

AMANDA SPENT the next two days rushing around, preparing for Josh's office party, helping Brandy with two other parties, moving into her new office, finishing the last of the shopping, and assuring herself that everything was wonderful between herself and Josh.

However, every time Josh jokingly called her his elf, she cringed.

And at his office party, she finally made up her mind.

It wasn't that things didn't go well. As a matter of fact, it was probably one of the best parties Amanda had ever organized. Even some of his family came, mingling with the business acquaintances, and oohing and aahing at the technology. Charmaine came with Wendell. "It's so connected to the universe," she exclaimed. She clung to Wendell's arm and looked up at him. "In a reality-based way of course."

"It's all so amazingly modern," Mimi said, while Judith admired the bathrooms and his mother admired everything.

"Your father would be so proud," she told him with tears in her eyes.

Even Josh seemed to be having a good time. He walked around, confidently explaining the technology to everyone. And he introduced Amanda to everybody. "This is the person responsible for all this," he'd say. "Amanda Kringleton. My very own Christmas elf."

When it was over, Josh was ecstatic. "We did it," he said to Amanda as they returned to his condo. "Hank says he's got people almost forcing their money on him." He led her over to the couch and pulled her down beside him. "This has worked out perfectly," he enthused as he stared at the Christmas tree. "I've got the investors lined up. We've got terrific personal presents for everyone." He chuckled. "You know, I haven't been this excited about Christmas since I was a kid. I can hardly wait for everyone to open their presents. I just hope they like them."

"They'll love them," Amanda said. "And the best part is, that you came up with most of them yourself."

Josh looked pleased. "I guess I did, didn't I?" He squeezed her shoulder. "But I couldn't have done it without my Christmas elf."

Amanda studied his features. "That is how you see me, isn't it? As your Christmas elf?"

"Of course," he said, obviously not getting the question. "My own personal Christmas elf."

Right, thought Amanda. She pushed herself to her feet, knowing the moment had arrived. "And speaking of elves, it's time for this one to go."

"Go?" Josh looked confused. "Where are you going?"

"The North Pole," Amanda reminded him. "That was our deal, remember? After Christmas, I'd go back to the North Pole."

Josh blinked twice. "Yes, but..."

"It's past midnight, Josh. It's Christmas Eve. On Christmas Eve, I'm supposed to go back to the North Pole."

"I know but..." He shoved a hand through his hair. "I didn't mean...that is, I didn't actually expect you to..."

"What did you expect, then?" Amanda asked. "I've done everything I was supposed to do," said Amanda. "We bought the gifts. They're all wrapped, and the gift tags are written. We had the office party. I played the part of your significant other." She put a hand on her stomach to stop the churning. "That's all I was hired to do, isn't it?"

Josh stared at her. "Yes, it is, but..."

"So you don't need a Christmas elf anymore?"

His gaze met hers. Then he lowered his eyelids. "I guess you're right," he said slowly.

Amanda's stomach sank with disappointment. She hadn't expected him to react any differently, but part of her had been hoping...

She drew in a long, deep breath. "Well, then," she said. "Thanks so much for everything. The office is fabulous. And you've done a lot for my business...not to mention my shopping skills. And I really enjoyed meeting your family."

"Yeah," Josh said. "So did I." He had a stunned look on his face, like someone who had just been run over by a truck and wasn't quite sure what was going on.

That was exactly the way Amanda felt. She kissed him on the cheek, picked up her coat, and walked out the door.

"I JUST DON'T GET IT," Brandy said.

She handed Amanda a cup of tea, sat down on a kitchen chair, and stared at her as if she'd lost her mind. "You broke up with him just because it was Christmas Eve?"

"We didn't exactly break up," said Amanda. "It just ended, that's all." She took a sip from the cup. "It was just a job and the job ended Christmas Eve."

"It wasn't just a job! You were practically living with the guy."

"I know."

"And it doesn't sound as if he wanted to break up."

Amanda recalled the stunned look on Josh's face when she'd walked out. "I don't think he did."

"So he didn't want to. You didn't want to." Brandy raised an eyebrow. "So why did you?"

"I had to," Amanda said. "It was going to end anyway." She drew in a breath. "And do you know how it would end, Brandy? He'd just stop calling. He'd get all involved in his work—he'd forget to call me—then he'd walk into his condo some evening and look surprised to see me there. He wouldn't mean to hurt me, but he would."

"This isn't hurting you? It looks awfully painful to me."

"It's better than the alternative." Amanda wiped back a fresh rush of tears. "I couldn't stand to hang around and watch him slowly discover that he doesn't need me."

"You don't know it would happen."

"Yes, I do." Amanda took another sip. "And so do you. You're the one who said people don't change."

"I might have been wrong," Brandy said. "I was wrong about Harvy."

"You weren't wrong about Josh," Amanda said. She took another sip of tea, but it didn't warm her. She felt cold inside, so cold she could have been at the North Pole.

11

"SATURDAY?" Josh said into the phone. "I don't know about Saturday, Mom, I'll have to..." An image of a small blond woman flashed through his mind. No, he didn't have to check with her anymore. "Yeah, okay," he said. "Saturday sounds fine."

"What about Amanda?" Edwina asked. "Do you think she'll..."

"No," said Josh. "Amanda will *not* be there."

There was dead silence from the other end of the phone. When Edwina finally did speak, her voice was filled with questions and concern. "We certainly haven't seen much of Amanda since before Christmas. It's the fifth of January. Surely she isn't still visiting her family?"

"I...wouldn't think so," Josh mumbled.

Edwina cleared her throat. "You two haven't... broken up, have you?"

"Not exactly," Josh muttered. They hadn't broken up. There wasn't anything to break up. It was a job that ended, that's all. "I'm just...not seeing her anymore."

"Why?" Edwina asked. Her tone sharpened. "You weren't cheating on her, were you?"

"Good God, no," said Josh. He couldn't imagine being with another woman.

"Then what..."

"I can't talk about this anymore," Josh interrupted. "I have to get back to work."

He hung up the phone and glowered at it. What was the matter with his family? They'd wanted him to have a relationship, and he'd had one. Okay, it hadn't really been a relationship, but they didn't know that. Why couldn't they just be happy he'd had one and forget about it? Then maybe he could forget about it!

That's what he wanted to happen. That's what he'd expected to happen. He'd forgotten about every other relationship in his life, including, at times, his family. But he couldn't seem to forget about his Christmas elf.

It had been two weeks since he had seen Amanda, and they'd been the worst two weeks of his life. When he'd woken up that first day without her there, his first instinct had been to phone her. But he'd been unable to think of a thing to say. She'd been right. The job had ended. He didn't have any more personal presents to get, or any more parties to plan. He didn't need a Christmas elf anymore.

He'd spent Christmas day walking around in a fog, watching his relatives open their presents, and listening to their praise and thanks. Naturally, they all asked after Amanda. "She's out of town," he'd told them. He didn't have the heart to ruin their Christmas by telling them the I'm-not-seeing-her-anymore story.

He'd thought after Christmas Amanda would slip out of his mind. That hadn't happened. He'd immersed himself in work. That hadn't helped, either. Nothing seemed to help. It was ridiculous. He seemed to have spent a good portion of his life forgetting about his relatives, and yet he couldn't forget about Amanda.

He picked up the photograph sitting on his desk. It was Amanda's Christmas present to him—a picture of his family. He ran a finger along it, pausing at his own face. The only person missing from it was Amanda.

Josh abruptly set down the picture, annoyed with everything and everyone in the world, and let out a bellow. "Mable!"

After a few minutes Mable stalked into the room. "What—"

"Do you have those technical specs I asked you to get?" Josh demanded before Mable could say a word.

"No, of course I don't. You just asked me for them ten minutes ago."

Josh glared at her. "I need them right now!"

"You need something right now, but it isn't technical manuals," Mable flung. "And if you bellow at me one more time I'm going to smack you over the head with my bottle of brandy." She came a few steps closer. "What's the matter with you, anyway? You've been in a lousy mood since Christmas. What happened? I thought you said your family liked their presents."

"They did like them." Josh smiled briefly at the memory of their enthusiastic responses. "They thought they were very thoughtful and very personal." His smile faded. They should have liked them. They'd been hand-picked by a Christmas elf.

"Then what's bothering you?" Mable demanded.

"Nothing is bothering me," Josh snapped, although to be perfectly honest everything bothered him. "It's cold outside. There's too much snow. And...and I just don't like January."

"Really?" Mable raised an eyebrow. "What do you want me to do about it? Get you a ticket to February?"

"No!" Josh snarled. He didn't think he'd like February much more than he liked January.

"Okay. Which month do you like?"

How about December? Josh thought. I liked December. "I don't know but I know it isn't this one."

"Perhaps it was December," Mable suggested gently.

Josh shoved a hand through his hair. "December wasn't bad."

"Oh, come on, Josh," Mable exclaimed. "You were happier in December than you've been in years. You only started getting miserable when Christmas came...and you broke up with Amanda."

"We did *not* break up," Josh snapped. "It was a job, that's all. It ended the way it was supposed to end—on Christmas Eve."

"Is that all Amanda was to you...an...employee?"

"Of course not," said Josh. "Amanda was more than that. She was...special."

"I think she thought you were special, too," Mable said. "As a matter of fact, for reasons that right now I'm hard-pressed to understand, I'd say that Amanda is in love with you."

"Really?" Josh felt a surge of elation that quickly died. "If she felt that way, why did she leave?"

"Because she didn't think you felt the same way."

"Of course I feel the same way," said Josh without thinking about it.

"Well, did you ever tell Amanda that?"

"No, of course not," said Josh. "How could I? I didn't know how I felt!"

"Well," said Mable, "now you do. What are you going to do about it?"

Then he picked up the phone. "The first thing I'm going to do is call my mother. I think she deserves to know the whole story." He grinned, suddenly filled with excited anticipation. "And then I'm going to get Amanda a very personal, thoughtful present." He took a deep breath. "I just hope she likes it."

"BUSINESS IS BOOMING," Brandy reported. "We won't have any problem paying the rent on this place for the rest of our lives—and paying ourselves a decent salary, as well."

"That's nice," Amanda said glumly. She wasn't sure she liked this office anymore. Every time she looked at it, it reminded her of Josh. Everything reminded her of Josh, from the snow on the windowpane to Brandy's face. She gave her head a shake. She'd cried all over her parents, and she'd cried all over Brandy, and it was time she got over this.

Brandy released a huge sigh. "Why don't you go home, Amanda?"

Because it's just as bad there, Amanda thought. As a matter of fact, it was worse. The place seemed empty without the clutter from the office, and Josh's relatives kept phoning and leaving messages on her machine. Amanda hadn't returned any of their calls.

The only person who hadn't phoned was Josh. Amanda hadn't really expected him to, but she couldn't help but hope that maybe he would.

She'd just arrived home and was in the process of making herself a cup of tea when someone rang her doorbell. When she opened it, she found Josh standing on the other side. His coat was open, showing his pink shirt, and his lack of a tie, his hair was mussed from the wind and probably his fingers, and just seeing him almost had her heart jumping out of her chest. For a moment neither of them said anything. Amanda couldn't think of a single thing to say and Josh just stared at her much the same way he had when they'd first met. Then he cleared his throat and gave her a small smile. "I'm staring, aren't I?" he asked.

"S-sort of," Amanda stammered. She peered over his shoulder, suddenly realizing that he appeared to have his entire family with him. "What…"

"I came to give you a Christmas present." He smiled faintly. "I know it's a little late, but I'm really hoping you'll like it."

"Oh." What? "You brought your family here, too so you could give me a Christmas present?"

"I had to," Josh explained. "They all helped me pick it out." He held up a hand. "I didn't intend for it to be a group activity, but…well, I told Mom the whole story and…she called Shelby and Shelby called Louise and Charmaine and…" He shrugged. "The next thing I knew, we were all there."

"Oh," Amanda said faintly. She had wanted him to spend more time with his family. She wasn't positive this was what she'd had in mind.

She opened the door wider. "Won't you…come in?"

"No, they won't," said Josh. He entered her apartment, closed the door and rested his back against it. "I will come in. They are going to wait in the coffee shop across the street. There are some things a man does without an audience and this happens to be one of them. We'll call them later.'' He hesitated with an uncertain look on his face. "At least, we might, depending on how this goes.''

Amanda waited for a moment in a vain attempt to lower her heart rate.

Josh pushed his hands into his pockets. "I should tell you that my family knows all about you.''

"All about me?'' Amanda said faintly.

"Yes. I told them the entire story.''

"You did?''

"Uh-huh.'' He winced. "They weren't very happy about it. My mother said I was reprehensible. Shelby told me I was a jerk. Marilla said it was a good thing I didn't have a cat because I'm too dense to take care of it. And Charmaine told me that I was the most cosmically unaware person she'd ever met.'' He sighed and bent his head. "And that was just the beginning.''

"Oh, dear.'' Why had he done that? And why was he telling her?

Josh raised his head and smiled faintly. "I think I might have deserved it. After all, hiring someone else to find out personal things about your family probably is something only a real jerk would do. And blackmailing someone into pretending we were involved is even worse.''

"Actually it was extortion,'' Amanda corrected. "And it seems to me I used the same tactics on you.'' She gave the door an apprehensive look. "Is that why your family was here? So they can tell me off, as well?'' She wouldn't blame them if they did, but she didn't think she was up to hearing it.

"Of course not!'' Josh reassured her. "I told them it was all my fault—which it was. I did sort of force you into doing it—although you didn't have to. I was going to offer to help out anyway."

"That's...uh...true," Amanda stuttered. "But does your family understand..."

"Don't worry. They're not mad at you or anything." His eyes gleamed at her. "They're not even that mad at me anymore. I pointed out that I was just trying to make them happy and give them what they wanted. That seemed to help."

Amanda wasn't surprised to hear that. Josh could soften up anyone with all that charm.

He took a deep breath, bent his head to study his hands and then looked back up at her. "Is that why you left me? Because you think I'm a jerk, too?"

Lord, she was crazy about him. "I didn't exactly leave you, Josh. The job just ended, that's all. I was your Christmas elf, and you said you wouldn't need an elf after Christmas."

"Actually you said that," said Josh. "And I thought you were right. You were right about everything else..." He frowned. "Well, practically everything else. I still don't think my mother would have liked a pasta maker."

"Maybe not, but..."

"You weren't right about this," said Josh. "I do need you. You would not believe how miserable I've been without you. I was even miserable during Christmas—even though everyone really liked their presents."

"Did they?"

"Uh-huh. They thought they were very thoughtful and very personal. Of course, they should have been. I had an elf to help me out."

There it was...that Christmas elf thing again. "Josh, I..."

"I've spent a lot of time thinking about this," said Josh. "And I've finally realized that I don't just need a Christmas elf for Christmas. I need one all year through...for ever and ever." He reached into his coat pocket, pulled out a box wrapped in cheerfully red Christmas wrapping and handed it to her. "If I tell you that I want you and I need you and I love you, and that I'll try very hard to get over being a jerk, do you think you might consider taking the job?"

Amanda was too stunned to take in what he was saying. She stared at him and then at the present. It was small and square and just the right size and... She looked questioningly up at him. "I think you should open that before you make up your mind," he said gently.

Was this actually happening? You shouldn't jump to conclusions with Josh Larkland, Amanda told herself a little hysterically. He could be giving *her* a pasta maker, and not offering her what she thought he might be offering, after all.

She removed the paper, opened the box and stared at the sparkling diamond. "Oh, Josh," she breathed. "It's...uh...I don't know what to say, I...I just..."

"Well, for God's sake, say something," Josh interrupted. "I'm going out of my mind here. Say 'yes,' 'no,' or 'Get out of here, you jerk' but don't just stand there because I can't..."

"Yes," Amanda said quickly. She smiled radiantly up at him. "Although I believe the proper response is 'Yes, thank you, I'd be delighted to...'"

"Terrific," said Josh. "I guess now we're officially engaged. And this time it's for real." He pulled her into his arms and up against him. "I'm glad that's settled. I thought I'd have to do a lot more groveling." He brushed his mouth against hers, then deepened the kiss. Amanda responded passionately, holding his head down to hers, reveling in the familiar feeling of his body, his lips, everything about him. "Oh, Josh, I love you so much," she whispered.

"I love you, too, Amanda," he mumbled. She started unbuttoning his shirt, then gave up on it, took his hand and started leading him down the hall. "Come on," she said. "I want to show you how us elves celebrate getting engaged."

They were halfway down the hall, still clutching each other, when Josh stopped. "What about my family?" he said. "They'll be waiting for us. Do you think we should…"

"Absolutely not," said Amanda.

There was a time for family. This wasn't one of them.

LOVE & LAUGHTER™

Jo Montgomery had her life planned out—a satisfying career, marriage with longtime boyfriend Alan Parish and definitely *NO KIDS!* Then she met gorgeous widower—and father—John Sterling. And Jo found out the hard way that:

Is a 4-Letter Word

(#35)–January 1998

For Alan Parish, being left at the altar was a blessing. Thank God he was still single! And since the honeymoon was paid for, what was wrong with inviting his friend Pam to enjoy it with him? But when the fictional honeymoon became fact, Alan discovered that:

Is a 4-Letter Word

(#37)–February 1998

Be sure to watch for these two hilarious romances by talented newcomer

Stephanie Bond

Available in January 1998 wherever Harlequin books are sold.

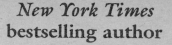

Christmastime...

When rediscovering
lost loves brings a
special comfort, and helping
to deliver a precious bundle
is a remarkable joy.

brings you gifts
of love and romance
from four talented
Harlequin authors.

A brand-new Christmas collection,
available at your favorite retail store
in November 1997.

HARLEQUIN®

The romance continues in four spin-off books.

Discover what destiny has in store when Lina, Arianna, Briana and Molly crack open their fortune cookies!

PAIN CAN BE THE MIDWIFE OF JOY

THIS CHILD IS MINE
Janice Kaiser
Superromance #761
October 1997

NEVER JUDGE A BOOK BY ITS COVER

DOUBLE TAKE
Janice Kaiser
Temptation #659
November 1997

DISCOVER YOUR DREAMS AND DISCOVER YOURSELF

THE DREAM WEDDING
M.J. Rodgers
Intrigue #445
December 1997

FOLLOW YOUR DREAM

JOE'S GIRL
Margaret St. George
American Romance #710
January 1998

Available wherever Harlequin books are sold.

HARLEQUIN®

Look us up on-line at: http://www.romance.net   FCSPIN

Born in the USA

Every month there's another title from one
of your favorite authors!

October 1997
Romeo in the Rain by Kasey Michaels
When Courtney Blackmun's daughter brought home Mr. Tall,
Dark and Handsome, Courtney wanted to send the young
matchmaker to her room! Of course, that meant the single
New Jersey mom would be left alone with the irresistibly
attractive Adam Richardson....

November 1997
Intrusive Man by Lass Small
Indiana's Hannah Calhoun had enough on her hands taking
care of her young son, and the last thing she needed was a
man complicating things—especially Max Simmons, the
gorgeous cop who had eased himself right into her little boy's
heart...and was making his way into hers.

December 1997
Crazy Like a Fox by Anne Stuart
Moving in with her deceased husband's—*eccentric*—family
in Louisiana meant a whole new life for Margaret Jaffrey and
her nine-year-old daughter. But the beautiful young widow
soon finds herself seduced by the slower pace and the much-
too-attractive cousin-in-law, Peter Andrew Jaffrey....

**BORN IN THE USA: Love, marriage—
and the pursuit of family!**

Available at your favorite retail outlet!

BUSA3